DEATH
on
DEMAND

DEATH
on
DEMAND

Kim Hill and
Owen Dale

THOMAS HORTON AND DAUGHTERS
26662 S. New Town Drive / Sun Lakes, AZ 85224

Library of Congress Catalog Card Number 85-80405

ISBN Number 0-913878-34-0
           0-913878-35-9

Printed by BOOKCRAFTERS

Typography by Spencer Graphics and Editorial Services

*For Joe, whose classes in economics
were truly "terms of endearment"*

One

Professor Joseph Birnoff smiled and stretched with pleasure—as much as a short, roundish man is able to stretch—in the back seat of the taxi. "Ah, Florida!" he mused to his companion. "Nothing like a tropical vacation at spring break, eh, Karl?"

His companion only grunted in response.

"Did you see those beaches from the airplane?" Birnoff continued. "Pure white sand. And the water! This place certainly deserves its name: Clearwater. I can tell already this'll be one of our most memorable vacations."

"Harump," the other man replied. "Just like Mexico City in 1976, I suppose. That was one tropical vacation I've done my best to forget."

"Well, I had a *great* time there," Birnoff shot back in quick defense. "And I told you not to eat that street vendor's tamales. It's not my fault you had to see so much of Mexico from your bathroom window.

"You're just grumpy because you don't like flying," Birnoff added.

"I don't like getting up at four in the morning to catch a plane."

"It was your idea to take that flight rather than the more direct one. How much was it we saved, as you kept reminding me before we made the reservations? About one hundred fifty dollars each, as I recall. You ought to be happy instead

1

of grumpy. You saved that one hundred fifty for only about two hours extra travel time."

"I am happy about that," Birnoff's companion replied. "If you think of that as income, it's a better hourly rate than the university pays me."

"So why are you grumpy then?" Birnoff demanded playfully.

"I'm not grumpy! I may like saving one hundred fifty dollars, but I hate getting up at four in the morning to do it."

"Well, that's the price you had to pay to save it. And it *was* your idea," Joe shot back. Then, in a whisper, he added, "And you are too grumpy." Joe cocked his head and, satisfied that his friend had not heard that last remark, went on in his normal tone of voice, "But enough of this. I'd rather talk about our trip, anyway. You're going to love this one, I'm certain. I've done my research thoroughly, as usual. You'll be able to play all the tennis you can possibly desire. And there's excellent swimming, golf, boating—all those sweaty attractions for you in the 'active set,' as I believe it's called. And there's fascinating local history, the prospect of some excellent company at our hotel, and a highly regarded cuisine to top it off."

"Everything you in the 'sedentary set' desire," Karl mused.

"All a matter of taste—"

"Please! Don't lecture me about differences in taste. After all, I'm an economist, too."

Birnoff blinked as if in surprise at being told some long-forgotten fact. "Yes, Professor Teasdale. Anything you say, Professor Teasdale," he joked. And then, more to himself than his colleague, he added, "Often wrong-headed, but an economist nonetheless."

Across the taxi seat Professor Karl Teasdale now stirred a little from what had seemed a sleepy—as well as grumpy—trance. Unlike his companion, Teasdale was a tall, lanky man who, in fact, looked a member of the "active set." Also unlike his companion, Teasdale was carefully dressed in a

2

lightweight sport coat, slacks, and coordinating knit shirt. Birnoff wore an old, rumpled business suit, a plain white shirt, and an out-of-date tie.

Teasdale squinted at the passing sights of palm trees, postcard-blue water, and bright sunlight. "Tennis courts, of course," he said. "Every resort has 'em. But how many? And in what condition?"

Birnoff smiled knowingly, assured now that Karl's interest was stirring from its usual postflight lethargy. "Let's see now, tennis courts, tennis courts," he said as he patted the pockets of his suit coat.

"They're hardly in your jacket," Teasdale offered dryly.

"No, not the tennis courts, but the brochure."

"What brochure?"

"About the hotel. Part of my research, you know."

Birnoff ran out of pockets to pat, frowned a moment in thought, and then concluded with a weak smile, "It must be in my bag."

"*One* of your bags," Teasdale corrected.

"Have to come prepared," Birnoff shot back as if defending himself on an old dispute. "One never knows—"

"Yes, I understand," Karl quickly cut in, as if the issue were a bit tired for him as well.

There was a moment of silence. Then Birnoff looked out at the passing city through first one window and then the other. "Well, Florida!" he concluded in obvious delight at what he saw.

"Joe?" his companion asked politely.

"Yes?"

"The tennis courts?"

"Oh, yes!" The plump man started. "Er, they slipped my mind."

Karl rolled his eyes.

"Have to try it from memory—without the brochure, of course. But I recall that the hotel has a tennis pro on staff. And an assistant pro and even a tennis pro shop. That all sounds to me like they take their tennis pretty seriously.

3

And it seems like there were four, or maybe six, courts. Er, would that sound about right?"

Without waiting for a reply he bubbled on. "It also seems they were made of something odd."

"Odd? Like concrete or clay, I suppose?"

"No, no. Something Oriental sounding. Like Chinese food."

Karl stared at the man in disbelief. "Tennis courts covered in Chinese food? Jesus, Joe, it's a good thing I've known you twenty years."

"Not covered *in* Chinese food," Joe replied archly. "Something named *like* Chinese food."

"I've got it!" Karl shouted. "Egg *Foo Young*! I've always wanted to play on Egg *Foo Young*. It gives great topspin, I'm told."

"No, it's something like *Shu Mai* or *Tar Hu* or *Har Gow*."

"Oh, I know," Karl laughed. "It's *Har-Tru*."

"That's it!"

Karl shook his head, still laughing. "That's one of those patented all-weather surfaces." He paused and then said, "Too bad. I really wanted to play on an Egg *Foo Young* court."

"Don't be so smug, Dr. Know-It-All. You don't, in fact, know it all, all the time either. Remember how I saved you from near-disastrous embarrassment in that restaurant in Paris two years ago?"

"That's not fair. People in Wisconsin don't eat *that* part of a pig."

"Nonetheless, just imagine what might have happened if I hadn't been there."

"Yes, yes."

"So without my vast culinary knowledge—"

"All right! *Touché*, dammit."

They rode on a few minutes without speaking until Teasdale was willing to break the silence with a conciliatory, "So tell me about this hot-shot hotel. The Biltmore, right?"

Joe's eyes lit up with the invitation. "The Belleview Biltmore," he corrected. "Known informally as 'The White Queen' because of the size and color of the building. It was built in the late 1890s as the Belleview Hotel. Some railroad magnate built it as the winter resort at the terminus of his north-south rail line to attract a rich northern clientele. In those days the very rich could come down in their private rail cars and park those cars, so to speak, right next to the hotel.

"The attractions then were much the same as those we'll enjoy on our trip: the chance to flee the cold northern winter for sun, surf, *tennis,* and sundry other pleasures in a relaxed, luxurious setting."

"Why's it now called the Biltmore?"

"It seems the hotel has changed ownership a few times over the years. At one time it was in the Biltmore chain, but that outfit went under in the 1930s. Yet that part of the name stuck."

"Have you seen pictures of this place?"

"Indeed. And the architecture alone is quite interesting. It's an impressive, rambling Victorian structure. The brochure says it's the largest occupied wooden structure in the world."

"Big deal," Karl shot back. "We get to stay in the world's largest one-hundred-year-old fire trap."

"Oh, no. The Army put in an elaborate sprinkler system. They used it for a barracks during World War II," Joe countered. And then, as if to justify his knowing this bit of esoterica, he added, "It said so in that brochure, wherever it is."

"Great," Karl mumbled to himself. "Now it's a hundred-year-old army barracks."

"It has a huge tiled swimming pool," Joe continued, "*two* full-sized golf courses—"

"*Two?*"

"Yes, they're big on golf."

"I suppose I could rent some clubs one day," Karl mumbled to himself. "But golf's one game I've never been able to master."

"And there's a cabana club," Joe continued, "with beachfront swimming facilities on an island just off shore. I guess I should have mentioned that the hotel itself is situated on a bluff overlooking Clearwater Bay and the Gulf of Mexico beyond. But, back on the list of things to do, there are organized card games like bridge, canasta, and backgammon and there's fishing, entertainment in the hotel, and quite a bit more."

"And you expect the food to be good?"

"I've been on a diet for three weeks. Need I say more?"

"That is a big sacrifice on your part," Karl agreed. "But I suppose all this luxury and entertainment are costing us quite a bit. In your usual custom you never sent me any details about the price of this hotel."

"It's not cheap, but we can afford it. We certainly did well with our new edition last year. Besides, as Birnoff's Fourth Law of Economics states: 'You get what you pay for—if you know what you're buying.' "

Karl grimaced and said, "How profound! I wonder if your students ever really understand your laws."

"It's all an effort to show them the everyday relevance of economics, you know."

At this point the taxi turned into a long, sweeping drive where a modest sign announced their hotel.

"Ah, this is it," Birnoff said.

"They were waved past a security guard at the entrance, and then their taxi passed a number of two-story houses— separate "cottages" for those guests who desired a high degree of privacy—and shortly pulled up before the main entrance of the hotel. It was, as Birnoff had said, impressive.

The building was a multistoried, multiwinged affair with the cluttered charm of overdone Victoriana. It was a jumble of intersecting, steeply pitched roofs, bay windows protruding here and there on every floor, and long, running verandas. The building was flanked on one side by the tennis

6

courts, on another by the golf courses, and on yet another by the pool and the dock for passage to the cabana club. Thus, the active guest was only a step or two away from his or her favored sport. And the entire assemblage was spread across a gently rolling bluff that allowed pleasant views of the Bay and Gulf. So, from the hotel or the golf course or the tennis courts or the pool, one always had a beachfront panorama as a visual backdrop. This panorama was, however, interrupted in its middle by a series of high-rise condominiums at the base of the bluff between the hotel and the Bay. This modern-day addition was a concession to economics over aesthetics, but at least it was only a modest one.

In short order the two men were delivered to the reception desk with their baggage—and mostly that of Birnoff, as his companion would quickly point out—flowing in an ill-matched train behind them. The clerk had to mask her surprise at the collection, but she managed to contain herself and greeted them with a professionally neutral, "Good afternoon, gentlemen."

"Good afternoon," Birnoff replied hesitantly while searching his pockets for something. "We have reservations and . . . and I've got the confirmation here somewhere."

"That's all right, sir. Just tell me the names."

"Oh, it's, uh . . . ," Birnoff mumbled as he continued to go through his pockets.

"Give up, Joe," Karl put in. "You probably packed the darn thing in your luggage. Lord knows it'd take a week to find it there." Then, turning to the clerk, Karl said, "The names are Birnoff and Teasdale. Professors Birnoff and Teasdale, that is."

The clerk rifled through a set of reservation cards and quickly came up with the ones she sought. "Ah, yes, here we are. Two singles for two weeks."

"Singles?" Teasdale reacted. "What's the daily rate?"

"These rooms are ninety-five dollars a night, sir."

"And what's a double go for?"

"Our standard doubles are one hundred thirty."

Teasdale turned to his colleague, who was doing a repeat of his earlier pocket-patting routine in search of the lost confirmation card. "Joe, did you hear that? The marginal cost of a double is less than half the cost of the second single. You probably didn't even investigate that, did you?"

Birnoff kept at his search, but he managed to reply, "Oh, I considered it."

"We should take a double, Joe. Why, over the entire two weeks we can save more than one week's cost at the single rate."

"Marginal benefit," Birnoff mumbled. Then he frowned, shrugged, and concluded, "I must have packed it. I bet it's in my briefcase."

"What?"

"In my briefcase, I said."

"No, not the confirmation. What did you say just before that?"

"Oh, that. I meant to say you were forgetting the marginal benefit. You know the rule: consume up to the point where marginal cost equals marginal benefit."

"So?"

"That means—in my calculus—that the marginal cost of the second single room is worth the marginal benefit of not having to stay in the same room with you."

"That's not nice! We've always done it before."

"Karl, I hate to tell you, but I suppose someone's got to. Over the years your snoring's gotten worse and worse. Two years ago in Paris I got almost no sleep."

Here Birnoff turned to the clerk and said, with surprising firmness, "Yes, it'll be two singles."

Two

The clerk smiled and agreed, "Very good, sir." She quickly finished the check-in and added, "If you gentlemen will wait just a moment, there'll be a bellman along to take you to your rooms."

The two professors nodded and then leaned nonchalantly against the check-in counter, Teasdale still mumbling to himself over the room rate and the revelation about his snoring. Birnoff, for his part, surveyed with pleasure the remainder of the lobby. The room was attractively furnished, but even more to the professor's liking, it exuded a quiet, dignified charm. Most of the guests, he surmised, must be hard at their self-appointed regimes of sporty fun. Only a few elderly couples had sought the tranquility of the lobby at this early afternoon hour.

That tranquility was, however, destroyed by the arrival of another guest. Or, perhaps, it's better to say a guest and his entourage. The main doors were suddenly flung open and a short, slightly fat man hurried in ahead of a crowd of bellmen and private porters carrying a caravan of luggage.

The new arrival struck a brief pose, head erect and arms akimbo, for just an instant after he entered the room. From that posture he scanned the lobby and, apparently seeing no one he knew (either to greet or simply to see him in his carefully chosen stance), he turned back to his minions. That brief pause was, however, long enough to give the two professors a good look at the man, and they shared an intrigued glance in response.

Professor Teasdale's inspection of the new arrival had gone from toe to head, his amazement increasing with each rising inch. Teasdale saw, first, slender Italian shoes made of something like white buck. Next there came the legs of a remarkable suit—canary yellow in color and closely fitted in cut—an altogether unfortunate choice in light of its wearer's lack of stature and his slightly bulging midsection. The man's shirt was soft brown, his tie white like the shoes. His suit coat was tossed over his shoulders like a cape. From his neck dangled white-framed "Arctic" glasses, and another pair of glasses with red frames were pushed atop the unruly mass of black curls that completed this amazing creature.

"All right, already," the man snapped in a thick New York accent. "Personal luggage to the desk, fellas. And the sample cases you can stack *neatly* in that corner. And remember, *be care-ful*, you're handling *art*." The last word came out in a long drawl, a New Yorker's approximation of a Southern accent.

Three matched and pristine pieces of Louis Vuitton luggage preceded the man to the desk. Even Birnoff paled when the latter were placed neatly alongside his own odd-lot pile.

"Hi, honey," the new arrival hailed the receptionist, still deep in his mock-Southern drawl. "How you-all been? How are the mint juleps and chitterlings?"

"Good afternoon, Mr. Farfel," she responded with a smile. "And how are you this year?"

"Simply pinin' for some fried chicken and iced tea, ma'am." But then, as suddenly as it had come, the hokey accent was gone, and the man asked in his original voice, "So, you got the rooms ready?"

"Everyone's confirmed, Mr. Farfel."

"Mrs. B's got her usual suite?"

"Yes, sir."

"And the meeting rooms?"

"I believe everything's just as you requested, Mr. Farfel. Your secretary took care of all the details."

"Yes, he's an efficient young thing, isn't he?"

While the clerk completed his check-in, Farfel looked about and spotted the two professors, both eyeing him curiously while trying not to appear that they were doing so. He looked them up and down quickly, spotted their luggage and grimaced, and then asked, "I don't suppose you're Lord Halsey's accountants? No doubt armed with grim numbers on our current cash flow, accounts receivable, and excessive consumption of toilet paper. And with brilliant ideas about how to boost revenues and lower costs?"

Teasdale and Birnoff looked at each other, entirely perplexed as to what the man was talking about.

But the desk clerk saved them. "Mr. Farfel, this is Professor Birnoff, and this is Professor Teasdale. They've just arrived for a vacation."

"Oh," the man replied. He brought the glasses on his head down to their appropriate place, inspected the two men again, and said, "Aaron J. Farfel of *Artworld* magazine. No offense, but in New York you'd be dead ringers for accountants."

"Oh, none taken, I guess," Karl replied dryly. And with a touch of something like fatigue, he added, "It happens all the time. Hard to say which profession would be more offended by the mistake."

"The bellman will be along in just a moment, Mr. Farfel," the clerk put in. "I'm afraid they're all occupied with putting away your file boxes and photograph cases."

"That's OK. Business before pleasure. Besides, I'm in no hurry. I'm on Southern time now. So tell me, though, who's arrived so far? Mrs. B?"

"No, sir. Her plane gets here about six."

"How about Cowboy Cal?"

"I beg your pardon, sir?"

"Mr. Caldwell, our 'good ole Texas buddy.'"

"Oh, yes, sir. Mr. and Mrs. Caldwell arrived this morning."

11

"And the evil Anglo-Saxon, Lord Halsey? Has he hit town yet?"

"Lord Halsey's party has been here a week already, Mr. Farfel."

"His party? A week already? Good God, they've come to lay siege to us. What or who's in this 'party' of the old boy's?"

"His wife, his chauffeur, and . . . ," here the receptionist smiled at the two professors before saying, "and some accountants on his staff."

"What'd I tell you fellas?" Farfel shot back at Karl and Joe. "I have a sixth sense for accountants. I knew they were about the place somewhere. They're probably lurking in the potted palms in the bar to see what goes on my expense account."

"Sounds like some accounting professors I've known," Karl mused.

"I assume, from all this discussion, Mr. Farfel, that you're not here on vacation," Joe ventured.

"It's all-out war, that's what it is. Or, well, let me put that another way. It's the annual shareholders' meeting of Arsgratia. That's not a household name, I know, but the firm owns and operates *Artworld* magazine, of which I'm the editor. Normally these meetings *are* something of a vacation. Oh, sure, there's always a little ritualistic handwringing about the past year's financial losses. But, hell, we're in this for art, right, not to become filthy rich."

"But this year it's different?" Joe led him on.

"You betcha. This year an 'outside party,' as *our* accountants like to say, is trying to buy up the interests of several limited partners so he can take over the partnership and magazine."

"And it's this British lord you just mentioned?" Karl asked.

"Yeah, Lord Peter Halsey. Surely you've heard of him. Europe's biggest pornographer. Or, maybe I should say the one who's made pornography semirespectable as well as outrageously profitable."

12

"Yes, now that you mention it," Karl agreed.

"Didn't *Time* do a story on him a few weeks back?" Joe began. "That's right. And I remember now, he's built his, uh, empire by buying up established newspapers and magazines and then, then—"

"Turning them into 'skin sheets' is the phrase I've found most appropriate," Farfel concluded for him.

"So you're afraid . . . ," Karl began.

Farfel nodded. "Academics aren't so slow as I thought. That's it exactly. If Halsey gets control, I'll be out of a job, art'll be out the window, and *Artworld* will be doing, pardon the phrase, 'spread' shots on nude artists at work, artists and their models, the history of erotic art, or, well, you get the idea. The possibilities are endless. The mind boggles at the thought."

"Hmm, so it seems," Karl agreed. "That would be a pity."

The bellman arrived to escort them to their rooms and, as a gesture of politeness, Karl added, "I wish you luck in your battle, Mr. Farfel."

"Yes," Joe added, "despite your distaste for them, I hope you have some clever accountants on your side. And some clever arguments, as well, to hold any wavering partners."

Farfel could only frown and shake his head in response.

*　*　*

Following their first-day-of-vacation custom, Joe and Karl met in the bar at seven for a celebratory bottle of champagne. As also was their custom, they first toasted another year's success of their economics textbook which made these biennial trips possible. And they played a favorite game of studying the other guests in the bar, speculating about their background and interests.

The two professors had done in both the bottle of champagne and, unknown to them, a goodly number of the room's other guests. At this point Karl was saying, "That fat lady over by the window, I bet she's—"

Just at that moment a tall, distinguished man approached their table and asked in an ever-so-proper British accent, "Look here, I don't suppose you're the accountant chaps from Touche Ross?"

The touch of exasperation in the man's voice would have been enough to irritate them, but being mistaken for accountants twice in one day was well beyond any economist's tolerance. The two men looked at each other, trying to decide whether they were angry or just embarrassed. Joe opened his mouth to speak but then shut it, not knowing what to say. He even looked down at his fresh attire—his old seersucker suit in place of the nondescript brown one he'd worn earlier—and thought: I must still be doing something wrong. He looked up at the imperious intruder, himself dressed in a silk shirt, ascot, and dark blazer, and thought further: On the subject of attire, what sort of *rara avis* is this?

It was Karl, however, assuming the haughty patrician air for which he was well known, who saved their pride by saying, "No, we are not the men from Touche Ross. Am I to conclude you're a Continental gigolo who's lost his companion?"

The man rocked back on his heels, clearly stung by the remark. He rocked forward, flushed a bit, and then, quite unexpectedly, roared with laughter.

"Oh, jolly super!" he said when he could control himself. "Damned fair of you, too. Bit cheeky, I was. Sorry about that."

The man looked down and saw their empty champagne bottle floating in the ice bucket. His eyes lit up and he said, "Look here, let me buy you another round. Could use a spot of the bubbly myself. Be a change to chat with someone with a sense of humor, as well."

The economists shrugged at each other as if to say, "Why not?" Following this cue, the man snapped his fingers at a waiter and pointed at the empty bottle. Then he sat down and took out a gold cigarette case. He offered the cigarettes around and, getting no takers, asked, "I hope you don't mind." Hardly waiting for their murmurs of assent, he lit up.

After taking a long drag, the man said, "Halsey. Peter Halsey. Delighted to meet you."

The two academics introduced themselves, and then Karl asked, "It's Lord Halsey, is it not?"

"Why, yes. How the devil did you know that?"

"We were talking with another man when we checked in today. He told us a little about you. Aaron Farfel, his name was."

"Farfel! Good Lord, I wager he had a packet of nasties to say about me. Beastly fellow, that. Good head for art, I'm told, but none for business. And he's rather . . . how should I put it, odd, don't you think?" Halsey took another drag on the cigarette and shook his head, evidently still thinking about Farfel.

Suddenly, Halsey's mind snapped on another thought and he said brightly, "I suppose Farfel gave you an earful about me. 'Pornography King of Europe.' Or the 'Blue Lord from Bath,' or some similar rubbish."

"He did mention the general orientation of your principal publishing ventures," Joe replied.

"The general orientation . . . ," Halsey started to repeat. Then he laughed again. "That's marvelous. Well, it's all true. I *am* the Pornography King of Europe. I *do* pander to the lascivious and the lustful that lurks in every man's—and woman's—heart. I do . . . well, must I go on? In short, gentlemen, I daresay I have simply recognized what is one of the most in-demand goods of all. And I provide a steady supply to meet the demand."

Karl and Joe smiled at each other, and Joe said, "That's quite astute. He could almost be an economist, too."

"Who was it that said," Karl mused, "that a parrot could be an economist if you only taught him to repeat 'supply' and 'demand'? I guess that means Lord Halsey qualifies."

"But as what?" Halsey shot back with good humor. "The parrot or the economist? All the same, if you fellows are economists yourselves, you must admit I was near correct when I guessed accountants."

The two men bristled at this remark, but Halsey did not notice. He did go on to say, however, "I expect that means you'd be able to understand clearly my position in this present business. Surely Farfel told you of that. A pornographer at a distance is no threat. But one up close, attempting to snatch one's baby, so to speak, for presumably illicit purposes . . . well, that's an entirely different matter."

"He was somewhat heated in his opinion of you," Joe agreed.

"And well he should be. I propose to take control of Arsgratia and that dreadfully run magazine of his. It's all part of my strategy to 'penetrate,' as my people say, the American market. You simply wouldn't believe their profit and loss figures at *Artworld*. And it's all such a missed opportunity. The name recognition that magazine has is extraordinary. That's something one could trade on most profitably."

"I presume," Karl said, "that *Artworld*'s poor profits are a reflection of their pursuit of other objectives."

"You mean the usually-honored-only-in-the-breach 'art for art's sake,' I suppose."

"Something like that, yes. After all, that's just what their company name suggests."

"To that I say one can have his art and that's all well and good. But this is, too, a business enterprise. And I ask you, must art and commerce be ever divorced?"

"I think you'd best ask Farfel that question," Joe observed.

"He's a hopeless case. A cultural Neanderthal, in fact, because he can't see the necessity of the marriage I've just proposed. Everyone assumes, as he does, that I'd turn his magazine into an arty *Penthouse*. But I recognize that the arts clientele of the magazine must continue to be served to ensure its success."

"But with a more liberal conception of what is art, I suppose?"

"Of course. And I'll freely admit that I see a good deal of art that pays homage to the beauty of the naked human form. Why, all the great masters painted nudes, did they not? It's merely a matter of recognizing that and giving that branch of art its proper representation in the magazine."

"I suppose one could view this like any other business takeover effort—of which we've certainly seen plenty lately," Karl said.

"That's just as I prefer it," Lord Halsey agreed. "It reduces to a question of business philosophy: How best can the interests of the owners be served? And I, for one, believe their primary interest to be in profits. And then, secondarily, how best can the given assets of the firm be utilized in pursuit of that primary interest?"

"I am surprised, I will say, to find an English peer so caught up in practical business matters," Joe ventured.

"My good man, your surprise is merely a product of the unfortunate and dated stereotypes in which you Americans have been soaked. Too much 'Upstairs, Downstairs,' 'Brideshead,' and the like. The 'telly,' I fear, has locked your conceptions of English society into what is, at best, a nineteenth-century caricature.

"We modern British have faced the necessity of coming to terms with contemporary economic realities—to touch on an area you must know professionally. I daresay that's what Mrs. Thatcher's all about, too. Even a peer—with the exception of the dwindling few *rentiers* among us—must face that accommodation. It merely happens that my *forte* is in publishing and cinema production. And, of course, that I am disposed to a particular branch of both those endeavors. Yet it all rests upon a firm grasp of the commercial prospects in those fields. And one must suppose it's rather a patriotic enterprise."

"Patriotic?" Joe reacted.

"Certainly. My individual commercial successes are—through the twentieth-century curses of progressive taxation and death duties—guarantors of the collective future of my countrymen. Can there be a nobler endeavor, I ask you?"

17

Joe would have replied had he thought of something sufficiently clever and had they not been interrupted by the arrival of a fourth person. But his mental lapse was covered when Lord Halsey rose and said, "Ah, gentlemen, my wife."

The two economists turned, and their reactions were much like those of everyone else in the bar. Joe nearly kicked over the cocktail table and Karl swallowed hard on his champagne, mumbling, "My word!" to himself.

The woman swept into the room like the film star they'd soon discover she was. She was tall, in fact very tall, very blonde, beautiful, and possessed of an amazingly well-endowed figure. And that figure was well-displayed to encourage amazement. She wore a dress that, from its low-cut top, hugged every curve on the way down to its thigh-high cut bottom. And she walked with the self-assured, feline-suggestive grace that only a few women can, or dare to, master.

The three men rose, Lord Halsey gracefully and the other two awkwardly. To her outstretched hand Halsey offered a gentle kiss, and in response the woman whispered something in a heavy German accent that sounded like "darlink."

Lord Halsey said, "Gentlemen, may I introduce my wife Helga. Helga, these are two American professors: Professor Birnoff and Professor Teasdale."

She coolly looked them up and down and said, "Charmed, don't you know. I am Helga. Perhaps, you have seen Helga in the cinema. *All* of Helga."

Karl choked again.

"Oh, so sorry," Helga murmured. "Vas it zee drink?"

"Wrong pipe," Karl coughed.

"You should drink more slow, yes?" she asked.

Karl agreed.

Turning to her husband, Helga said, while playfully dusting some imagined lint from his collar, "Darlink, Helga had zee most awful game of tennis. Zee balls, they would not go anywhere Helga wished."

"That is a rare problem for you," her husband agreed.

"You're a tennis player?" Karl ventured now that he could talk again.

"Yes, but of course. But Helga is only, how you say, an amateur at *that*. Are you playing zee tennis, also?"

"Why, eh, yes."

"We shall play, then. Perhaps tomorrow, yes? Helga can use all zee practice she gets. Call Helga, darlink, and we have a game."

Three

"Young man, are you blocking the sun intentionally or is it, I trust, that you are simply unaware you are doing so?"

Joe Birnoff blinked in surprised reaction to the question. He turned and saw the elderly lady whose morning sunlight he had blocked. Joe had just walked onto one of the hotel's terraces where this woman was enjoying tea and a newspaper in the early morning sun. He was shocked and a little titillated in reaction to her imperious question. It had been years, maybe decades, since anyone had called him "young man." The greeting left him entirely speechless.

Joe shifted the magazine he carried from under one arm to the other, squinted at the sun to see how it fell across the lady's table, and then attempted to reply. "Er, uh, I'm sorry. I just . . ." The thought of being considered a young man still left him tongue-tied and unable to finish his sentence.

The woman, for her part, was altogether under control. She needed only an instant to "size up" Birnoff: His confusion in response to her remark. His eccentric attire which included a well-aged Izod shirt, once red when bought years ago while such items were fashionable in America the first time, now only pink and frayed, as well. And there were the equally ancient chino slacks whose barrel-straight legs exaggerated Joe's shortness and stoutness into something like a clown-suit caricature. In contrast to these old garments, there were his brand-new, shocking-blue-and-red jogging shoes. (More of the clown suit, the lady might have been led to think.) And there was the newly purchased copy of *Artworld* magazine under his arm.

The woman studied him an instant over the frames of her glasses and she may have clucked to herself in deprecating response, perhaps to say "what an altogether unfortunate appearing person" or perhaps instead "yes, I know *this* type well." Nevertheless, something about Birnoff snared her attention and, carefully putting down the teacup that had been equally carefully poised before her lips, she said, "I infer that to induce you to move I must invite you to sit and have some morning tea."

Such an invitation must also have been a rare thing for Joe. He looked quickly from side to side to make certain he was the recipient of this offer. He started to reply, but his attempt was muddled by the giddiness of thinking of himself as a young man, "Well, I would . . . that is to say—"

"Oh, don't dither so," the woman calmly interrupted. "Sit down." She caught a waiter's eye with a practiced waiter-catching flick of her hand and pointed to the teapot for a refill. Then she folded and put aside the newspaper she'd been reading. As the woman did so, Birnoff was becoming sufficiently conscious to study her and do some of his own typecasting.

She was somewhere in her mid-sixties so, in truth, she did have ten to fifteen years on Joe. She was not, strictly speaking, a beautiful woman and perhaps she had never been, but she was attractive in an old-fashioned sort of way. At least that was how Birnoff thought of it. In addition, her dress, her makeup, her manner, and—as Joe put it to himself— her remarkable state of physical preservation for her age all gave testimony to a life of wealth and ease. Her body was slender, firm, and erect. Her skin was taut. Her hair had a luster and fullness that, even if it came from a bottle, Joe was certain it would have been a very expensive bottle. Her suit—and it was a business suit despite the fact that this was after all a resort hotel—was conservative and simply cut. But it was at the same time stylish and distinctive, a far cry

21

from the carbon-copy blue suits Joe had seen almost exclusively on women before: worn by female corporate recruiters who came to interview identically attired female students at Oberlin College for postgraduation jobs.

Having rearranged her table and ordered tea, the woman turned to Joe to say, "I am Ann Neal Bertram of Boston. I come to this hotel often, but I do not believe we have met."

Joe wrinkled his brow, perhaps because his brain was at least unconsciously probing where he might have heard this name before. But conscious and subconscious did not connect, so he only replied, "I'm Joseph P. Birnoff. Of Oberlin, Ohio. And this is my first visit to the Belleview. It's a beautiful place."

"Are you a connoisseur of art, Mr. Birnoff?" she asked, carefully pronouncing the word in quite proper French. "Do they have art in Ohio?"

"Art? Why, no. Er, that is *I'm* not an art connoisseur. But there is art in Ohio. At least I believe there is."

"But you are reading an art magazine," Mrs. Bertram replied.

"Oh, that! I met the editor yesterday. Here at the hotel, in fact. So when I went to buy a newspaper this morning and saw this copy among the magazines at the newsstand . . . well, I thought I'd take a peek at it."

"The editor, you say," Mrs. Bertram replied as she poured more tea. "What's his name? I just might know the man."

"It was Farfel. Aaron Farfel, I believe."

"A New Yorker?" she asked.

"I believe so."

"A short, plump man?"

"Yes."

"I see," she concluded with a twinkle in her eye.

She paused as if to see if Joe had anything of his own to add about Farfel, but nothing was forthcoming. Then, glancing across the terrace to hide her amusement, Mrs. Bertram asked, "So tell me, Mr. Birnoff, what do you think of this magazine and its art? You sound as if you might have about the average American's interest in serious art. What, dare I use the phrase, does the—and I mean nothing personal by this—'average American' think of such art?"

Joe turned his head as if cocking an ear to make certain he'd heard right. He wasn't sure whether he should be offended, but he judged by the woman's voice and inflection that he should not. "Well, I'm actually not certain yet," he replied. "I've only flipped through the magazine a little. Although I must confess that much of the abstract, modern art I saw there is ... uh, beyond my appreciation, I suppose I should say."

"It is highly regarded by some, you know. And it is often quite expensive."

"Yes, I can understand that from a professional standpoint even though I can't appreciate it as art myself. You see, I'm an economist and I have a theory about the value of such items."

"An economist's perspective on art! How intriguing." Mrs. Bertram was obviously quite interested by this thought. "Do elaborate on that, will you, er, Dr. Birnoff, I presume?"

Joe beamed. Not only was she interested in economics— which made her a rare person outside his profession—she was astute enough to infer his professional title, as well. He cleared his throat, a bad sign as his students knew, for this effort usually presaged a long-winded reply, and said, "Well, the high prices that some art objects command reflect, in part, the tax benefits of investing in art and then donating it to charity at an appreciated value. Then, too, art has a certain snob appeal. High prices force more people out of the market, making ownership more exclusive and prestigious. The result is an exception to the law of demand, since higher prices can create greater demand for these goods. We call that the Veblen effect."

Mrs. Bertram toyed with her cup, musing over his explanation for almost a full minute after he was finished. At last she said, "That's quite astute, Dr. Birnoff. And it certainly coincides with my own observations. I really must deceive you no longer. For while Aaron Farfel is the editor of the magazine you hold, I am its founder and the general partner in the company which owns it."

"I inferred something like that," Joe said with restrained pride. "Mr. Farfel mentioned your name yesterday, as I've just recalled." Subconscious and conscious had at last made connection.

Mrs. Bertram might have reacted to this revelation, but her mind had clearly skipped ahead to another thought. She was silent a moment, phrasing her thoughts, before saying, "Your economist's perspective on art intrigues me, Dr. Birnoff. You might be able to provide me—from that point of view—some useful thoughts toward a difficult business matter I face."

"I wager it's this business takeover attempt," Joe guessed.

"My, my," Mrs. Bertram responded and studied the professor more closely over the top of her glasses. "You *are* astute, aren't you? Either that or Aaron was his characteristically talkative self when you met. Might I suppose that you can even anticipate my specific question?"

"After talking to Mr. Farfel, I suspect I can. But let me get the facts in order first. You, I presume, are the major shareholder in the corporation which controls the magazine."

"In fact, it is a limited partnership. I am the general, or controlling, partner and there are almost a dozen limited partners."

"I see," Joe replied. "Then this Briton, Lord Halsey, wants to take control by buying out either you or enough of the limited partners so that—"

"So that he could have me voted out as general partner," she concluded for him.

"And you won't sell, of course."

"Of course."

"So you face the task of maintaining the confidence of the other partners."

"Precisely."

24

"And where Lord Halsey dangles the prospect of great profits before them, you are seeking an alternative benefit to induce them to remain loyal."

Mrs. Bertram took off her glasses in astonishment. "My word, that's it exactly! But if you are clever enough to see my problem so clearly, do you see its solution as well?"

Here the professor unconsciously raised his arms in a half-flapping, half-shrugging gesture. What he did, more precisely, was to stretch out his arms to pull his nonexistent shirt sleeves out of his nonexistent suit coat. He was puzzling out the problem in his head, and this was one of his problem-puzzling gestures. A close and intimate observer would even have noticed a few more of the professor's similar gestures. Even Mrs. Bertram caught the odd wrinkling of his brow and the scratching at an ear that did not itch. She only missed the funny way the short man danced his legs from his chair, his feet barely touching the terrace floor.

But at last he spoke. "I suppose there are a couple of approaches open to you; however, the way I see it, your best one would be to remind the other partners that the magazine was formed to promote interest in art and, in that light, it has been highly successful. Sheer economic return was not the originating motive and should not be used now as an excuse to sell out. The return on their investment is measured in satisfaction for having founded a highly respected publication. Thus their return would be called 'in-kind' instead of 'in-cash.' Economists also refer to this as psychic income." The professor appeared to have finished, but after a brief pause and another flap of his arms, he added, "You might even remind them that art has very often been subsidized by other economic activities and that their publication is, then, a worthy example in a long and prestigious tradition of support for the arts."

Joe had the habit, when speaking of economic matters like this, of appearing to talk to a spot in the air before him rather than to the person he addressed. (Some said he was actually reading his thoughts off some imagined blackboard in the sky.) Yet had he been more attentive to his breakfast companion, he would have said she nodded in all the right places. And when he was finished, she replied, "Yes, that makes good sense to me. I suppose my own thinking has developed along similar lines, but you have expressed it so much more precisely. By using your arguments perhaps I can make the case more forcefully now."

Again the professor beamed with satisfaction. The lady was not only an interested, but an appreciative pupil.

★　★　★

Karl was all smiles at lunch. "Joe," he gloated, "you should have seen my backhand this morning. Even *you* would have appreciated it. And my topspin was as good as ever. Despite the winter layoff, my game's hardly lost a thing."

"So you've had a good morning?" Birnoff asked, smug from satisfaction with his own activities so far this day.

"First rate. I slept late, for me at least. I had a bracing early morning swim. I had my tea and toast at poolside. And I was still able to present myself to the tennis pro early enough to get paired for a demanding game of singles. *And* it turned out I had not only a good opponent, but an interesting one, as well. She's the wife of some Texas oilman. But the best part . . . oh, but that's a long story. Before I get into that, how's been your morning?"

"Entirely satisfactory, as well," Joe replied. "I strolled on the grounds, getting the lay of the land, you know. I took the boat to the cabana club on Sand Key—that's the adjacent island I told you about—to assess the swimming there. Back at the hotel I started a new novel by the pool and read for a good hour. And . . . ," here Joe paused for effect, "and before all that I had breakfast with the general partner of the company that owns that art magazine Mr. Farfel told us about yesterday."

Karl's jaw dropped. "No!" he said in surprise.

"Indeed. We had a pleasant little talk about this business takeover attempt. I believe I suggested one or two ideas which may prove useful to her in the fight."

"That's amazing!" Karl interjected.

"I hardly think that's fair," Joe sniffed. "After all, we Keynesians do concern ourselves occasionally with practical concerns just as—"

"No, no, that's not what I meant," Karl interrupted. "What's amazing is the coincidence."

"The coincidence?"

"Yes. My tennis opponent this morning—the wife of the oilman—she's a partner in this company, too. Caldwell's her name. Mary Margaret Caldwell."

"And you talked of the takeover fight?"

"Yes. After our game we fell into the inevitable what-are-you-doing-here kind of discussion and she sort of poured it all out. Evidently this fight with Halsey has become an all-consuming problem for some of these people."

"So this Caldwell woman is resisting Halsey's offer, as well?" Joe asked.

"So it seems. She's an old friend of the general partner, Mrs. Bertram. That must be the one you talked with. They met at Vassar when Mary Margaret was a student and Mrs. Bertram a rich alum involved in fund raising at the college. They became close friends and stayed in touch over the years, especially because of a mutual interest in art. Then they were both involved in starting this magazine about five years ago. Did Mrs. Bertram mention her to you?"

"No, she only said there were about a dozen other limited partners, and I inferred she was concerned that some of them would give in to Halsey. But she didn't say which ones."

"That's much the way Mary Margaret described the situation, too. She said the partners have their first business meeting this afternoon. That's when they'll get last year's financial statement."

"And when they'll begin to see who's firm and who's wavering in the takeover fight," Joe surmised.

The two men fell to thinking—each in his separate mental world—about the implications of this takeover struggle. And they might have spent the remainder of the lunch in this fashion except that Joe still had one unasked question for his friend. Presently, he roused himself from his own thoughts to ask of Karl, "I suppose you offered your opinion to this Caldwell woman about how they could resist Halsey's takeover bid."

"You do recall that one of my fields in graduate school was business finance," Karl shot back.

"So it was," Joe mused. "Let me see now, just what period was that, anyway. Probably around the publication of the first edition of Hunt, Williams, and Donaldson. I wonder if that would qualify as the pre-historic period of business finance?"

"It was merely the same time when you were learning your macroeconomics from the first edition of Samuelson, I believe."

"It was not! It was the second edition," Joe said in defense of his age. "But what was your advice to her? I'd like to compare it with my own."

"I told her that, in general, one ought to look at this as a question of tax sheltering."

"That's just where I expected you'd begin. I can imagine the rest of your argument, as well, but why don't you give me its high points so I can tell if I'm correct."

"It's really quite simple," Karl began. "Given the marginal tax rates of some of the partners, the tax-sheltering effects of the accounting losses of the magazine could save taxable income from other sources. On an after-tax basis, they would be better off than if the magazine made a modest profit. Some of them may need this tax benefit explained to them, of course. And if this approach does not sit well with some partners, then the others could offer to buy them out, creating a modest bidding war. I don't believe that 'greenlining' and 'golden parachutes' will be significant problems in this case."

Karl crossed his arms and smiled with satisfaction over this argument. And then, in conclusion to his explanation, he added, "The woman was so taken with my ideas that she invited the two of us to dine with her and her husband tonight. She's eager to report to me the effects of my argument when she's tried it out on the other partners."

Four

"That's all much as I expected you'd argue," Joe concluded.

"No doubt you took another angle," Karl replied. "Probably based on some mushy argument about the value of the warm, fuzzy glow all those partners should get from sponsoring this critically acclaimed but financially unsound artistic venture."

"Of course. And despite your sarcasm, it is a valid economic perspective. But enough of this shoptalk. Let's move on to a really important subject, like dessert."

"You know it's Tuesday. I only eat dessert on Monday, Wednesday, and Friday."

"Oh, yes. But is it your waistline or your pocketbook that's responsible for this routine? Never mind, I'm ordering the ice cream cake with fudge sauce. We can plan our afternoon while I eat it."

Joe hailed a waiter and ordered the dessert, and then he turned back to Karl to ask, "I don't suppose you'll want to 'jock it up,' as they say, this afternoon after swimming and tennis this morning?"

"No, I'd better not push myself. I've had a three-month layoff since winter set in in Madison. But I'm certain I'll be ready for more tennis tomorrow morning. Of course, I could be tempted by some deep-sea fishing if the hotel can arrange that."

"Ah, the decisions life forces upon us," Joe agreed. "I felt that way about lunch. Would it be the 'London Broil Chasseur' or the 'Seafood Crepes Bonne Femme.' But, like you and your sports, I decided there's always tomorrow for what I pass up today."

"I'm sometimes surprised you don't have both at once," Karl said. "But enough about food, what's our program for the afternoon?"

"We've a couple of options. We could go ahead and rent a car and start our customary touring of the area. Or we could be lazy and stay around the hotel. There'll be card games beginning at one or two o'clock. And there are the pool and the beach for soaking up some of this famous Florida sunshine. Any preferences?"

"I suppose you might twist my arm and get me to submit to a rubber of bridge," Karl offered. "That is, if there are any other competent players about. I'm sure that would make you happy."

"I don't think I'm quite ready for bridge yet. That'd require more mental effort than I can manage this early in vacation. I prefer the idea of lounging on the beach myself."

"So you can show off your tan when you get back to Oberlin?"

"Tan fat is better than pale fat, I always say," Joe replied.

"Oh, why not. I suppose a spring break tan isn't such a bad idea. We full professors must keep up the image of wealth and leisure, right? Especially for all those junior faculty who are spending their spring break holed up in the library."

"I did wonder what our deans might think," Joe replied. "But what the heck, we are tenured *and* full professors, as you say."

A few minutes later Joe and Karl were ambling toward the boat launch for the cabana club. And they offered a curious and amusing sight to the other guests in the vicinity. Birnoff alone was quite a spectacle—in his ill-matched Hawaiian-print shirt and oversized swimming trunks.

31

Souvenirs of a trip to the islands with Karl, he'd tell anyone who might ask. Together with a narrow-brimmed straw hat and plastic "flip-flop" shower shoes, Joe's outfit alone was remarkable, to say the least. Karl, for his part, was dressed in his usually careful way: with a well-fitted terry cloth robe over a matched shirt-and-swimsuit combination. But the robe was a bit long and it gave him the look of a monk in a shrunken habit. He and his oddly attired colleague were an eye-stopping duo.

They had taken a long and out-of-the-way path to the boat dock, walking first in the opposite direction and then returning along the edge of the bay-front bluffs on which the hotel was sited. Joe had suggested the route so he could point out the bay-side vistas he'd discovered on his morning hike over the area. They were about to round the corner of one of the high-rise condos to take in a particularly good view from its deserted back side when they almost bumped into Lord Halsey. The man had just turned the corner in front of them and was charging along in their direction, head down and with a fat briefcase in each hand.

"Hullo!" he shouted in surprise. And then, after absorbing the visual shock of seeing the two men's attire, he asked, "My word, are we off to the ruddy beach?"

"Hello, Lord Halsey," Karl replied, choosing to ignore the slight either to his sartorial taste or that of his friend which was evident in the Briton's eyes.

"Oh, call me Peter. I've had more of this 'your Lordship this' and 'your Lordship that' than I am quite able to tolerate. You Yanks are amazingly awed by titles for a supposedly democratic people."

"Pure envy, that's all," Joe put in. "Just ask any member of the Republican party." Joe took a sideways peek at his companion's reaction to this remark, but Karl ignored him to ask of Halsey, "You look like you're headed for work, not play, yourself. You do remember this is a resort hotel?"

"Some of us must work for a living," Halsey laughed. "Those Arsgratia people are having their first business meeting today. I'm not entirely optimistic that they'll let me in, but I'll be sitting outside the door, presentation in hand, so to speak, on the odd chance that they do."

"It looks like you've got quite a presentation there," Karl agreed, eyeing the briefcases.

"I'm ready for any counterargument. My staff have spent two months putting all this together. I even have something of a war room—just a separate apartment, really—in this high-rise."

"Are your personal rooms here, too?" Karl asked with a critical glance at the building. "These places look a bit conventional compared with the hotel itself."

"Good lord, no. Why, I'm in the Duke of Windsor suite in the hotel. A nice touch, what? But I keep this apartment to have a quiet place to work mornings. And it's got a super view of the water, wouldn't you agree?" Here Halsey raised one briefcase-laden arm to gesture toward the bay. "I've even sent all my people back to London now," he continued. "It's all up to my powers of persuasion and my dazzling plans for the future of *Artworld* magazine." Here Halsey nodded to one of the briefcases. "At this point I sink or swim, as they say, on my own. It's the personal touch, don't you know?"

Halsey paused and something caught his eye. Glancing up at the high-rise building he smiled. "Ha, there's Helga," he said. "You fellows might be just in time for quite a show."

The two professors looked up to see Helga's naked back as she leaned against the railing of a fifth-floor apartment balcony. A half-curtain of beach towels draped over the steel railing of the balcony obscured the rest of her body. She was brushing out her long hair, tossing the locks back to dangle over the balcony with each pass of the brush.

"Helga has taken to using the apartment in the afternoon when I'm finished with my morning work. The balcony up there is the only place she can sunbathe nude. You Americans really are a bit touchy about that, you know."

33

Halsey stared up at his wife's back for almost a full minute, then he shook his head and started to say, "I'm afraid you're out of luck—"

At just that moment a blond, boyishly handsome young man came through the sliding glass door on the fifth-floor terrace. He, too, was naked, at least from the waist up, as they could see over the towel-curtain, and he walked out to accept a torrid embrace from Helga.

Halsey had been turning back to face the professors, and neither was certain he'd seen the young man. But his voice went flat as he completed his sentence, "she's not going to turn around."

There was a little pause of either embarrassment or indecision, then Halsey looked at his watch and mumbled, "Must be on my way, I fear. Nose to the grindstone and all that, what?" He hurried off toward the hotel.

After a glance at the now-empty apartment terrace, the two professors watched the Briton's slowly receding profile.

"That was the assistant tennis pro," Karl said to Halsey's distant back. "I met him this morning. Some college kid they've taken on for the season."

"I trust he's just working on her forehand," Joe quipped.

*   *   *

Calvin Caldwell was enjoying himself enormously. The rich Texas oilman, husband of Karl's tennis partner of the morning, leaned back in his chair in the hotel dining room and grinned. "Professors, huh?" He laughed a playfully contemptuous laugh. "Of economics to boot!" Again he laughed.

Mary Margaret Caldwell cleared her throat nervously and said, "Yes, Cal. Professor Teasdale teaches at the University of Wisconsin. And Professor Birnoff's at Oberlin College in Ohio. Those are both quite good schools."

Karl frowned inwardly and looked around the room, trying to imagine he was dining at someone else's table. God, if he tells us how far he's gotten in business without any economics . . . Karl let the thought trail away, unable to stomach whatever would be required to complete it.

Joe Birnoff blinked like a sleepy owl, but his vacant look masked his own reaction to Caldwell. He probably sees us as stereotypes, Joe thought. In our cheap suits and with our bumbling manner. But this guy's a Hollywood caricature himself.

And there was some truth in Birnoff's assessment. The fiftyish Texan was big, muscular for his age, and sun-chapped, brown, and leathery in complexion. He wore a western-styled business suit. And, believe it or not, as Joe mused to himself, the man actually wore cowboy boots and a Rolex watch. They must have made him check his Stetson at the coatroom, Joe concluded.

But Caldwell *was* having a good time. "So they're still trying to teach economics in the colleges? Amazing. I learned mine in the oil fields. And cutting deals for land or cattle or cotton in the back of a pickup truck. By the time I owned my first company—I was twenty-five then—I was making up my own economics as I went along. And it's worked, too. I wonder if any of your college students have done half as well."

Caldwell folded his arms and rocked back in his chair. Had he known the phrase, he might have gone so far as to add, there, I've thrown down the gauntlet. What can you possibly say in response?

Karl let out a low, barely audible sigh. As he reached for his drink, he joked, "At least it keeps us middle-aged professors off the streets."

Joe blinked again and thought to himself, darn that Karl! I can see he's not in the mood for this. But someone's got to stand up for the profession or we'll be taking this guff all evening.

"We aren't attempting to train business entrepreneurs like yourself, Mr. Caldwell," Joe began.

"Call me Cal, Doc. So what are they supposed to be, armchair businessmen?"

"Well ..., Cal, we're not, strictly speaking, trying to train people for any business profession. That's the goal of our colleagues in business administration."

"Oh, yeah. The guys that gave us the MBA mentality," Caldwell put in. "They turn out cocky kids in button-down shirts who want to start at thirty thousand a year to read their computer printouts, talk about management by objectives, and take long lunches, but who don't want to roll up their sleeves and do any real work."

"Calvin," the man's wife said with as much sternness as she could muster against her strong-willed husband. And she put her hand on his arm to restrain him further.

"But those aren't economics students," Joe persevered.

"Just what do you economists teach then?" Caldwell demanded.

"I'm certain you don't want a dissertation on that subject," Joe began, "and as a famous member of our profession once said, every short statement about economics is misleading. Nonetheless, I think it fair to begin by saying simply that economics is concerned with the allocation of scarce resources amongst competing ends. Beyond that, economists study individual and collective behavior in the production, allocation, and consumption of goods and services. It is wisdom about such matters that we hope to impart to our students. Wisdom that might be applied to their individual lives, their professions, and to their evaluations of public sector economic policies."

"The allocation of scarce resources," Caldwell repeated. "Amongst competing ends," he went on. "And individual and collective behavior, as well," he added. He considered all this a moment and said, "Oh, I get it, ivory tower intellectual sort of stuff. That explains why practical businessmen like me can get by without any economics."

Joe wanted to launch into a brief list of the practical applications of his discipline—in business, in government, and even in the average person's everyday life—but Caldwell's wife beat him to the rebuttal.

36

"Well, I for one would have been glad to have an ivory-tower intellectual at our business meeting today," Mary Margaret volunteered. "Professor Teasdale, I tried to make the arguments you suggested this morning, but I didn't seem to make any headway with the other partners. There was a lot of disagreement, some quite heated argument, but surprisingly little progress on the decisions we were supposed to make. It seemed everyone had his own different opinion of what should be done. Most of us—except Calvin here, of course—are amateurs in business anyway. I fear we're too ignorant of economics to see our way clearly."

At last Karl decided to enter the fray. "I am surprised, therefore," he began, "that Calvin didn't sort out all the problems based on his—how was it you put it—practical businessman's knowledge."

But Caldwell was not to be bested. "It's not my job to solve the problems of this messed up business," he snorted.

"Calvin's only a partner to appease me," Mary Margaret quickly explained. "We hold our share jointly and, I have to admit, just because of my interest in art and my friendship with Mrs. Bertram." She paused to smile at her husband and then added, "Calvin only suffers through these meetings to keep me happy."

"And," Caldwell added, "because I can use the tax loss."

"Yes, I expected someone among the partners would be in this more for the tax losses than anything else," Karl agreed.

"But we're in it for the sake of art," Mary Margaret protested.

"*You're* in it for art," her husband corrected. "I'm involved to keep you happy. *And* for the tax loss."

Joe shook his head sadly at this remark.

"Hell, Doc," Caldwell said in quick response to the gesture. "A good businessman has to do things like that today with this screwy tax system of ours."

"Entirely true," Karl agreed. "But that's a subject for another discussion. I'm increasingly interested in the plight of Arsgratia and how it will be resolved. I must say, as well,

Mary Margaret, that the quandary you describe among the partners—that is, of being ignorant of economics and even their own best economic interests—is hardly a unique one. I fear much of the American public is similarly ignorant."

"But how can we all be so ignorant?" Mary Margaret asked. "Why, take our little group of partners. Most of them are college graduates." Here her husband snorted in derision, but she ignored him to continue. "They're all successful in their individual professional pursuits—admittedly, mostly in the art world. But I'm not certain we even had a rational discussion of our financial problems today."

"Ah, rationality!" Joe repeated, as if someone had pushed a secret button that turned him on like a child's motorized toy.

"Don't complicate this any more than we must, Joe," his colleague murmured. Turning back to his hostess, Karl continued, "It's the product of inadequate economics education from kindergarten through high school."

"But not in college, I suppose?" their host quipped.

"Few universities require their students to take a course in economics, so we only get the opportunity to work with a minority of the students."

"Not that we all do such a great job of teaching even those students, or in trying to educate the general public for that matter," Joe interjected.

"Yes, I fear we economists must shoulder part of the blame here, as well."

"But you could solve all these problems, right?" Caldwell probed. "All we'd have to do is handle it your way."

Karl ignored the sarcasm to go on, "I do believe I see the root of the problem. If the public was instructed in just a few basic economic principles, we would have made considerable headway."

"But, Professor . . . ," Mary Margaret began. She blushed, paused, and then almost stammered on, "I'm embarrassed to admit it, but . . . I had a course in economics at Vassar years ago. I remember about supply and demand and things like that. But that didn't help me today."

"Mere buzzwords devoid of intellectual content," Karl concluded. "At least as you probably remember them now. Or, I suppose one could say," and here Karl laughed to himself, "a parrot's repetition of what are to him meaningless sounds. Those are, in fact, key concepts in economics to be sure, but what you really need to understand are the principles that lie behind such concepts. Take, as an example, what has come to be rather crudely referred to as the TANSTAAFL principle."

"The what?" Mary Margaret asked.

"TANSTAAFL," he repeated and then spelled the acronym for her. "That stands for 'There Ain't No Such Thing As A Free Lunch.'"

"That's economics I can understand," Calvin put in.

"It's also Birnoff's Second Law of Economics," Joe interjected.

Karl frowned at his colleague's remark, but then he replied, with a touch of his well-known condescension, to Calvin, "I expected you would."

"It doesn't sound very . . . very . . . ," Mary Margaret did not know how to conclude.

"Erudite? Academic? No, I agree. It is a bit common, but it suggests an important notion. That is, that at any given time there are simply not enough resources to satisfy all wants."

"So?"

"So some opportunities must be sacrificed to satisfy others. Economists call those foregone actions opportunity costs, and the development of *that* concept led to the formulation of the supply curve."

"And what, I suppose we must ask, led to the demand curve?" Caldwell queried, perhaps with the hope that doing so would get them through the entire discussion that much more quickly.

"Careful," Karl warned. "You might end up remembering some of this stuff. But the answer is the Law of Diminishing Marginal Utility. That means that succeeding units of the same good yield decreasing amounts of satisfaction to the user. Imagine, if you will, your reaction to playing two, three, or four hours of bridge. Even for my card-playing colleague here, the Law of Diminishing Marginal Utility would still hold. Each additional hour would bring successively less pleasure. In Joe's case the effect might begin to take hold a little later than with the rest of us, but it would still operate."

"So how do we get to the demand curve from there?" Mary Margaret asked.

"Because to induce someone to consume more of a given good, the price must be lowered, and lowered, et cetera. You see the relationship, of course. If the price did not fall, the individual would not be willing to buy the next game of bridge—to continue with the same example—because his satisfaction per unit of dollar expended is also falling."

"Of course," Caldwell agreed wearily. "Does that mean that the longer you talk, the less of your meal I'm gonna have to pay for?"

"Calvin!" his wife scolded. And then of Karl she asked, "Are there any more of these laws?"

"Well, uh, yes, several," Karl replied uneasily, fearful now that his host could have been serious. "But maybe I'll just mention the Law of Diminishing Returns."

"I think I know that one," Mary Margaret responded. "That means it takes more and more to produce less and less."

Her husband laughed again and asked in a whispered aside, "I wonder if that applies to instruction in economics?"

"That's not quite it," Karl replied to his hostess, fortunately not having heard Calvin's query. "It means that as the use of one resource is increased in producing some good or service while holding the use of the other resources constant, the amount of output will increase, but by smaller and smaller amounts."

"Why is that law important?"

"It leads to the conclusion that to induce someone to produce more and more of a given good, the price must be successively increased. And, conversely, to *discourage* production of a good, one would reduce the price received by the producer. Thus prices and the willingness and ability to produce go hand in hand."

Karl decided it wise to end his little lecture, and the table fell quiet with Mary Margaret pondering his remarks, Calvin silently thanking whichever deity he thought responsible for this turn, and Joe concentrating exclusively on his food. But Mary Margaret was troubled by some of her reflections on what he'd said and she soon asked, "Don't you find it somehow . . . somehow crass that economic behavior as you've just described it is based only on self-interest?"

"It's like the rest of life, isn't it? People seek pleasure and avoid pain. It's the most natural of behavioral principles."

"It still seems . . . well, crass."

" 'Crass' is not an economic concept."

"Perhaps it should be," Mary Margaret concluded.

Five

Joe Birnoff squinted. It was too good to be true. But there it was: an almost certain grand slam bridge hand, just in what cards he alone held. If only his partner, the slightly deaf, peroxide-blue septuagenarian across the table, didn't blow it in the bidding.

"Two hearts," Joe bid for an opener.

The woman on his left cocked a curious eye at Joe without turning her head. She probably thinks I'm an amateur with an ordinary hand, he mused.

"Pass," the woman bid, and Joe sighed with relief.

His partner hesitated. She started to bid, changed her mind, and then with prim firmness said, "Two spades," as if that's what she'd had in mind all along.

God, Joe thought. I feared she was about to say clubs.

"Pass," the man on his right announced, looking up uneasily at his own partner.

"Four clubs," Joe quickly followed. I'm halfway home, he thought. Wait'll Karl hears about this hand.

Before the woman on his left could decide on her next bid, however, the sleepy calm of the hotel lobby was broken by the sound of a door being violently slammed open down one of the nearby halls. Following that, a wave of noise—of mingled shouts, of angry cries, and of breaking furniture—washed down the hall. The scattering of people in the lobby froze for an instant.

Then those frozen postures were rocked by another wave of the same noises, clearly discernible now as men fighting. And the second wave broke the shock induced by the first. Suddenly porters, desk clerks, and odd guests were running to see what this commotion was about. Joe's bridge foursome held firm against this countertide for a moment, but they had all turned in response to the noise. Joe could even see old peroxide-blue wavering in indecision, perhaps trying to determine just what it was that was filtering into her half-deaf world.

Joe clenched his cards more tightly, stared at the table, and mumbled, "Probably just a scuffle among the staff. The bid's to you, I believe," he added to his neighbor.

But the din rose in volume. A pair of old men dozing nearby finally stirred and ran—or, rather, trotted in the lame and shambling fashion of old men—down the hall. And the latter break overwhelmed Joe's foursome. Old Blue half rose, said something vaguely like, "Well, I never," and dropped her cards to follow the two men.

Joe sputtered and waved a hand after her, but to no avail. The other two players were hot on her heels as the growing crowd of spectators added to the clamor.

Joe sat alone, staring at his hand, the dream of a perfect grand slam flashing and then fading before his eyes. "Damn," he said quite aloud, and then he sighed in resignation. A beaten man, he rose and walked slowly down the hall, still gripping his cards absentmindedly.

When he reached the scene of the commotion, Joe edged into the crowd of onlookers to where he could peer over the heads of two tittering housemaids. What he saw jolted him out of his disappointment over the card game. There in the middle of the floor was Aaron Farfel screaming at and striking awkward blows at Lord Peter Halsey. Despite his pugilistic ineptitude, Farfel was attacking with considerable vigor. But the stronger Briton, though bruised and disarrayed, was beginning to get the better of his opponent. Both of them were, alternately, swinging punches, tearing at clothing, and calling the other names.

A third man was struggling to get hold of Halsey and restrain him. And one of the male hotel clerks was attempting to wrestle the squirming Farfel out of the fray. Immediately behind the main participants Mary Margaret Caldwell was shouting like a distraught schoolteacher whose charges had at last succumbed to the anarchy just beneath their cherubic surface. Mrs. Bertram was there, too, more restrained but still visibly disturbed, saying again and again, "Gentlemen, please." And in the midst of a cluster of other people, near the door to the meeting room from which this fight had spilled out, stood Calvin Caldwell laughing heartily.

The two men were shortly separated, but they strained and wrestled against the arms that held them apart.

"Bastard!" Farfel screamed. "I'll tear your throat out."

And Halsey countered with an equally angry reply, inviting Farfel even to attempt such an effort.

Mrs. Bertram was whispering to some of the other men from the meeting, and a pair of them moved to assist in dragging Farfel from the scene. Another approached Halsey and began to whisper to him, presumably trying to reason him into calm.

The noise of battle had now receded, and there only remained the gossipy murmur of the crowd of spectators. Mrs. Bertram, not acknowledging these people directly but clearly sensing their presence, squared her suit jacket and passed a hand across her head in search of errant wisps of hair. Reassured of her personal decorum, she spoke commandingly over the noise, "Arsgratia partners, I believe it wise to adjourn until tomorrow. Shall we meet at two o'clock to discuss Lord Halsey's proposals?"

The partners accepted this question as more of an order and began collecting their purses and briefcases from the meeting room. The crowd, too, was breaking up, some to follow one or the other of the fighters—perhaps in the hope the struggle would be re-engaged elsewhere, some to return to their earlier pursuits, and some to edge to the door of the meeting room and peer inside, hoping to discern the reason

44

for the scuffle. In this jostling and shuffling of bodies Joe suddenly found himself alongside Mary Margaret Caldwell. She was exhausted from her own anguish over the fight and, seeing Birnoff, sighed, "Oh, Professor, wasn't it awful?"

"Whatever precipitated this . . . this?" Joe asked as delicately as he could.

The woman sighed again as if to catch her breath. "It was Halsey," she said. "Or, rather, his presentation to the partners. He had some perfectly awful things to say about Aaron's editorial decisions and how they've ballooned our losses. Aaron began to argue with him and then, then after they'd exchanged a few words . . . well, Aaron practically dived across the table at the man. Halsey staggered back against the door and Aaron went after him again. That's when the doors gave way and they fell into the hall."

"My word!" Joe was truly shocked. His experience with even the most conflictual of departmental faculty meetings had not prepared him for anything quite like this.

About that time Calvin Caldwell ambled up, hands stuffed in his pockets, still smiling to himself over the melee. "Quite a show, huh, Doc? I didn't think the little fairy had it in him."

"I gather that Mr. Farfel—I trust that's who you mean—was quite provoked by Halsey's presentation to the partners."

"Provoked? Farfel would have killed him on the spot if he could've. The only problem was that his hands are about as far from lethal weapons as my wife's. Hell, in fact, Mary Margaret would have been a tough match for the Brit. All those years of country club tennis, you know."

Mary Margaret frowned but held back whatever reaction went through her mind.

"Just like in the old days of the oil industry," Caldwell reminisced. "I've seen a lot of business deals settled by the 'fists and blood' approach in my day."

"Did you ever participate in any of those deals?" Joe asked, pretending to keep up the conversation as he tried to sort out the other partners as they drifted away.

"A few. Won 'em all, too," Caldwell boasted. "Still in all . . . ," and here his voice turned serious and, as a consequence, caught Birnoff's attention again. "We had a saying in the oil fields that a man whose only business skills were in his fists wouldn't be long in the business."

"I don't believe I—" Joe began.

"Halsey's nailed him," Caldwell explained. "And with sound business arguments. At least for those who want a return on their money out of this Sunday School operation, Halsey destroyed him in there. The choice is to keep Farfel and his hopeless ways—along with my tax losses—or to chart a whole new course and begin to make some bucks. So . . . when you've got no business legs to stand on, *and* you can't do any better with your fists than old Aaron, boy you're in a heap of, uh, trouble, as we oil men say when our wives are around."

"But to oust Farfel," Joe began to ask, thinking over this conclusion, "to oust Farfel I presume they must oust Mrs. Bertram, too."

"Yes, that's right," Mary Margaret agreed, and her voice cracked as she did so.

*　*　*

Karl Teasdale, as some might say, cut a respectable figure on the tennis courts. His regulation whites revealed a lean, almost muscular physique that would have been the envy of most men his age. And Karl was no duffer. His game was creditable and his competitiveness intense. Karl on the court gave a wholly different impression than did Karl at the lecture podium, for example.

Had Professor Teasdale been a womanizer and had he chosen to use his tennis court assets to assist his womanizing, he surely would have been a great success among that segment of college coeds who, for reasons either of curiosity or improved grade point averages, find it desirable to pursue handsome older professors. But Karl Teasdale was not a womanizer. True, he was not entirely uninterested in women. But having remained a bachelor, in part simply by fate, well into his middle age, Karl had accustomed himself to a life with little female companionship.

True, as well, Karl thought of himself as a clever and engaging fellow—when he chose to be—with the women he occasionally met socially. But two circumstances limited his experience with and interest in women. One of these was the fastidiousness that confirmed bachelors of either sex seem inevitably to develop, a fastidiousness that leaves such people exceptionally particular about just whom of the opposite sex they will even deign to spend an hour with at a cocktail party, take out to dinner, or, should matters reach such a state, let sleep over in the sanctified privacy of their homes.

The second circumstance was the limited range of Karl's experience with women. Not being one who required regular female companionship, Karl had always been content to satisfy whatever were his needs in that quarter within the limited confines of the university. Thus, it was at Sunday afternoon sherry parties given by the dean's wife or at postgame dinners hosted by one or another faculty member, or on very rare occasions at dinners at a sorority house that Karl Teasdale met the few women he knew. Thus it would also be no surprise that Karl knew few types of women.

There was, in his experience, first the modal female faculty member: long on serious academic matters (and sometimes known to be long-winded about them, as well) but short on fashion consciousness or, for that matter, feminine charm. She carried purses as big as shopping bags; wore only sensible, flat shoes; and, like her male counterparts, wore clothing that was out of style or never had any in the first place. She was just fine, even Karl would have said, for a Dutch-treat dinner to argue about the current state of the economy and its short- or long-term prospects. But for female companionship in the usual sense of the word, no, the modal female faculty member just wouldn't do. She was just too . . . too . . . Karl never could decide exactly what. Maybe just too serious. Or too professional. Or maybe just too plain. No, if the modal female faculty member were Karl's only prospect for an evening of entertainment, he would just as soon stay home and read a little Emily Dickinson.

Then there was the modal faculty wife: burdened with the responsibilities of a couple of children to feed and clothe and an aging house to maintain on her husband's always inadequate salary. And burdened, as well, with the self-imposed guilt that she should have done better with her life. After all, hadn't she gone to Berkeley or Chicago or Duke, too? Hadn't she dreamed of graduate school or a career in medicine or law or business, as well? But someone had to work to pay the bills when hubby got accepted at a prestigious graduate program first. And someone had to bear the children, and cook the meals, and . . . and the list went on, as Karl knew all too well from too many cocktail party conversations with too many modal faculty wives. Bitter, that's what she was. The modal faculty wife was bitter in the life in which she was trapped. And she was seldom fit company even for a brief conversation at one of those obligatory faculty social affairs.

And then there was the modal female student. Although with this last group Karl no longer thought in terms of modalities. For he would lump all college women together with no need for discrimination. Pretty or plain, intelligent or slow-witted, aggressive or shy, they all shared the same fatal flaw for Karl: they were children. Developmental biologists had missed an important distinction, Karl liked to argue to his similarly aged colleagues. Perhaps the human body was mature by age eighteen. But the brain, he'd say, even at twenty-one or twenty-two, was still invariably adolescent. It was a wonder they were allowed in college at all in this condition, and recognition of it should force the college professor to rethink what he could even hope to achieve with such ill-developed mental capacities.

For Karl, then, college women—or "girls" as he preferred to say—were a group to be suffered or, preferably, ignored—

at least on a social basis. In truth, he could never think of them as women, and it was beyond his imagination how a mature male could derive any but the basest physical pleasure from their company.

Thus it was that Karl Teasdale was unprepared in every respect for Helga. For Helga was a woman not plain like the modal female faculty member, not trapped in and ever ready to bemoan a boring life like the modal faculty wife, and certainly not an adolescent in mind or body like the modal college coed. Helga was, instead, a beautiful woman who lived a decidedly uncommon and exciting life and who knew how to squeeze every ounce of pleasure from it in the most adult of ways.

And Karl was especially unprepared for Helga when they met on the tennis court. While his colleague was savoring the prospects of a grand slam at the bridge table, Karl was waiting outside the pro shop to get paired for a game of singles. Head down and racquet clasped between his thighs, Karl was busy retying his shoelaces in one of those new, unconventional ways that was supposed to add two points to your game or make you walk on the proper side of your foot or . . . or something Karl couldn't remember but thought he should try anyway. Should he get a partner who was into such fads, Karl wanted it to be clear that he knew all about them, too.

Suddenly someone grasped the racket handle that stuck out behind his legs and, giving it a firm upward push, induced Karl to bolt upright and rise up on his toes in involuntary reaction.

"What the—" he cried.

"Why it is Herr Professor!" The prankster was Helga.

For a moment Karl didn't think she was going to let go of the racket. She looked up and down his half-turned body, smiled mischievously, and then let him down ever so slowly. "I give you the rise, yes, Herr Professor?" she asked.

Karl was rattled. "Uh, lady, . . . that is, Helga. I'm surprised to see—"

49

"You are playing zee tennis today, Professor?" she asked, cutting in. "I, too, am playing. But my usual partner is having his days off today. I have no one to play with." The last line came out like a sad sex-kitten's pout.

And the line had its intended effect on Karl: he wilted. That is, most of him wilted. But Helga could have simply stood around the court, saying nothing, and she would likely have had the same effect. Her tennis attire, one might have said, left everything to be desired.

Helga, too, was in regulation white. But that was where she and tennis etiquette parted. Her top was a clingy, low-cut, spaghetti-strapped little number that, as Karl would soon learn, seemed to turn transparent with the least blush of perspiration. It had, as well, the briefest of flounces to cover her bottom. And when the flounce bounced, as only Helga could make it bounce, it revealed the briefest of bikini pants that completed her outrageous outfit. Karl took all this in in a single, mind-numbing glance. But he couldn't have so much as guessed how Helga tied *her* laces.

"Would you like to play with me, Herr Professor?" she purred in a low, almost conspiratorial voice as she watched his eyes go down her body.

Karl stammered, "Play?"

"We begin with zee tennis, yes, Herr Professor?"

"Er, tennis? Why, yes. Just, eh, call me Karl, that is."

"Oh, but of course, Herr Professor Karl." She took his arm and guided him toward one of the courts.

"Yes, we begin with zee tennis," she concluded. Still clutching his arm, she asked, "Are you the kind of man who likes to go first, Herr Karl, or should I?"

"Go . . . go first?"

"Why, yes. With zee serve, of course."

*   *   *

Aaron Farfel was just about "in his cups," as the saying goes. Slouching low on one elbow, his chin barely above the

50

top of the cocktail glass before him, the man sat disconso-
lately at the bar of the Garden Seat restaurant, a popular es-
tablishment near the hotel. Joe and Karl—out on the town
in search of local culture and cuisine—were both struck by
his air of dejection, evident from his posture alone, when
they were shown into the bar to await their table.

Karl's usual reserve would have allowed him merely to
observe Farfel's plight and then proceed directly to his own
table. But something in what Karl had often called his
friend's "mushy liberal makeup" induced Joe to stop and
greet the man.

"Good evening, Mr. Farfel," Joe hailed, as cheerfully as
possible. "Here to dine?"

Farfel turned his head just far enough to survey Joe with
a single, sad eye. Then he said, "Nah, just to drink."

"I understand the food's quite good. 'Locally popular,' I
believe the guidebooks say of the place. You wouldn't care
to join us, would you?"

"To eat?" Farfel quickly replied. He appeared to be considering the idea from a mental vantage point somewhere between
glum disinterest and outright hostility. But Joe's insistent
smile and his obvious good intentions forced the man to respond at least slightly in kind. "Nah, I'm drinking my dinner
tonight. But if you care to join me, pull up some bar stools.
I'll buy you drinks and we'll toast the way the world turns."

Joe turned to Karl and, ignoring his friend's obvious consternation, motioned to a stool. When the two men settled
onto their stools on either side of Farfel, his head went up
and he looked quickly from one to the other and muttered,
"Jeez, it's an invasion. I'll tell you fellas one thing, though.
It's a damn good thing you're *not* accountants. I'd probably
strangle you both after what some accountant's homework
did to me today."

"Yes, I heard about that," Joe agreed sympathetically.
"But you mustn't give up yet. The partners might still support you. After all, there *are* other things in the world besides profits."

51

Farfel cast a wary look at Birnoff, glanced at Joe's colleague with equal suspicion, and then asked of Karl, "Is he sick or what? Jeez, you should of seen those people's eyes light up the more Halsey talked about all the money they could make."

"Odd, is it not, how powerful the profit motive is?" Karl mused.

"But surely many of them entered into this partnership for other reasons in the first place," Joe continued. "How was it you put it the other day? Art for art's sake, wasn't it?"

"Yeah, that was five years ago when we first started. Funny how support for that noble idea has eroded after five years of looking at business in the red."

"Well, there's the more prosaic—and also profitable in a different sense—position of Calvin Caldwell."

Here Farfel cocked a questioning eye, and Joe explained, "He told us he was in it for the tax write-off based on the losses."

"Maybe he knows more about how to manipulate the tax system than the rest of us," Farfel concluded.

Joe suddenly began to pat his pockets and, not finding what he sought there, added, "Something you said a moment ago gives me an idea. A counterproposal you could make. And it arises precisely because the partners heard an accountant's and not an economist's point of view today. If I only had a pen and pad"—here he paused to recheck his pockets—"I'd draw you a little diagram. Oh, but let me explain it without the graphics.

"You see, accountants are terrible about looking only at the short run. Their stock in trade, of course, is information about the *past* performance of a firm. You know, balance sheets and profit and loss statements. All stuff about where the firm is at a single point in time or about how it fared *last* year."

"Yeah, how I know," Farfel interjected.

"But we economists emphasize that the future might be quite different from the past. For that matter, in thinking of

52

the future one must also distinguish between the short and the long run. Now it seems to me that you could argue Halsey is offering a proposal that will be profitable only in the short run. And you could say that his argument about what would happen under your continued editorship is based on the simple projection of past performance into the future with no change in policies or objectives.

"You see, the novelty of what Halsey wants to do might make the magazine quite popular and successful in the short run. But, I ask you, could it have a long-run future?"

Joe had appeared to pose this question to the empty space between him and the wall behind the bar. Farfel did a little double-take at this gesture and, confused, turned to Karl. The latter man simply touched Farfel's arm as if to say, just wait a minute. Sure enough, when his mental wheels had turned a bit further, Joe answered his own question.

"Well, I say that perhaps it would not. After the novelty had passed, I wager that the old, serious art readers of the magazine would find it too shallow and insufficiently sophisticated to suit their tastes. After all, Halsey's strategy implies a popularization, if you'll accept that term, of the magazine's content.

"But what of the newer readers?" Joe continued with his one-man question-and-answer monologue, "those attracted to the magazine because of its, shall we say, racy content."

"Yeah, what of 'em?" Farfel demanded, seemingly because he was getting even further "into his cups" and wanted to challenge the professor's rhetorical style.

"I venture the hypothesis that they, too, after a time, would find the magazine of decreasing interest. If it's simply raciness they desire, *Playboy* and *Penthouse* and their kin will always deliver more. The art that remained in the magazine would probably bore these readers, just as the, uh, other stuff would offend the serious art reader. Thus, you see, I'm sure, the argument to set against Halsey's."

"Uh, I'm sure," Farfel said rather uncertainly. He blinked and stared back at Birnoff, waiting for further explanation.

"It's simply the short- versus the long-run perspective," Joe concluded with something like pride of authorship. "Convince them to take their short-run losses for the tax advantages they provide, and then argue that you'll pursue some long-run profit strategies appropriate to a serious art magazine. You need only juxtapose that position against the false promise of Halsey's, that would attempt to create a magazine for many interests that, in the long run, would appeal to none."

Farfel swayed on his stool as he rethought this argument. Then he mumbled, "Juxtapose. Yeah, I should juxtapose a blunt instrument against the side of Halsey's head. Then maybe we could really lay his threat to rest."

Six

The next day was a busy one. It began with Karl and Joe finding Mrs. Bertram alone in the breakfast room at a quite early hour.

"Couldn't sleep," she explained with a weak smile after inviting the two men to join her. "I fear I cannot eat either," she added, glancing at the toast and tea growing cold before her.

"Worried about your business meeting today?" Joe asked cautiously.

"Quite frankly, yes. At times I've even believed myself beyond worry and on the verge of resignation. I'm afraid Lord Halsey's won."

"But the fight with Mr. Farfel yesterday?" Joe protested.

"I fear that was Aaron's pitiful attempt to lash out—when he saw Halsey was winning over the majority of the partners. From some points of view I'm certain Halsey's was a brilliant presentation yesterday."

"How about the Caldwells?" Karl asked. "Do you think they were convinced?"

Mrs. Bertram answered absentmindedly, still preoccupied with some last thought of her own. "No, they'll remain firm. Mary Margaret would do anything for me, I'm certain. And Calvin?" Here she paused and looked up, seemingly puzzled by just what to say about the man. Then she answered her own question. "I don't think Calvin really cares about the business. I suppose he's just in it to appease Mary Margaret. Satisfying her whim, he'd probably say. At our meetings, he just sits there grinning, watching the rest of us argue and fight ... year after year. But he'll do whatever Mary Margaret wants to do."

She paused and stared into empty space, leaving her companions feeling a bit awkward and unsure about what to say next. Then she took her napkin from her lap and folded it slowly and carefully, pursing her lips as she studied her own movements.

Joe Birnoff, watching from the corner of his eye, thought that for the first time he could see signs of the woman's age—there was an awkward hesitation in her movements, a quivering shake in her hands—signs he had not noticed in the more resolute and in-control Mrs. Bertram he had met the first morning at the hotel. Maybe she was beaten. And because she knew it, her pride and her mastery of her bearing were slipping away.

But the woman had some hidden reserves. She drew herself up squarely and looked to one and then the other of her breakfast companions. "I still have one last opportunity to succeed," she said with her old authority. "One must play that hand for all it is worth, and then ... then, even if we lose we'll have gone down fighting."

She rose, and the two men half rose with her. She frowned at the gesture, perhaps because she feared it more for her age than her sex. Then she said, looking again from one man to the other, "Wish me luck. I'm certain I shall need it." And with that last remark, she departed.

Looking after the woman and shaking his head, Joe concluded, "It's too bad. I really feel sorry for her." After a pause, he added, "This may have ruined my appetite, as well."

Karl raised an eyebrow in surprise at the last remark, but his thoughts, too, were mostly on Mrs. Bertram. "Who was it that said there's no place in business for sentimentality? I ought to know, but I don't. Maybe Frederick Taylor?"

"More like Silas Marner or Uriah Heap," Joe cracked. "Or perhaps it was Herbert Hoover. It sounds like a Republican-party platform plank, as well. But then, I suppose it's an idea with international appeal. I'm certain Lord Halsey would agree with it."

"Yet if one believes in the profit motive, and I trust that even you still lecture on that in your classes, it's good to see proof of it in the real world. Even if we find some of its interpersonal consequences unfortunate."

"Of course I believe in the profit motive," Joe shot back. "But I also believe in other motives that drive human behavior."

"You are not, however, a businessman about to take control of an ailing concern to 'turn it around' into a money-making venture."

"True. But there's no certainty that Lord Halsey will be able to turn it around either, assuming he does get control of the company. He might even destroy the reputation of the magazine and still not produce a profit."

"Well, speaking of the devil," Karl interrupted. "I suppose we could give the devil his due."

Joe followed Karl's eyes to discover Halsey at the door of the restaurant waiting for a table.

"You said yourself that your appetite was already spoiled," Karl continued. "For the sake of my curiosity, let's push it a little further." Karl then caught Halsey's eye with a wave and motioned the man toward their table.

"Hullo, hullo. Top of the morning to all," the man greeted them cheerily.

Harump, Joe thought to himself. He wanted to ask: Do you people really say that, or is it just one of my TV stereotypes of Britons? But he decided the question was too nasty and, by saying nothing, he submitted to Karl's asking Halsey to join them.

"You're certainly the picture of happiness this morning," Joe ventured, hoping he might deflate the man by means of a rear instead of a frontal assault.

"Indeed, and with every reason to be so, what? I sense victory, gentlemen. Rather like Wellington at Waterloo. It's said he foresaw his triumph, you know."

"I've always been suspicious of fortune-telling military men, or even businessmen, for that matter," Joe said in a quiet but audible aside.

Karl frowned at his colleague to silence him. But Halsey's spirits were not to be dampened. He may not even have heard Joe's remark, for he continued in his buoyantly enthusiastic way, "Ah, yes, it's very close now. But there's much work yet to be done. A man needs a proper breakfast for that," he added, taking up a menu to study. While reading, he went on to say, "My final presentation to the Arsgratia partners is this afternoon, and I must be entirely prepared. In addition, I may face my toughest challenge at mid-day." Here he paused for effect, glancing at the two men to be certain they were listening. "That Caldwell chap—you know, the Texan—he rang up last night. Wants to have a little 'pow-wow, Texas style,' as he put it."

Karl and Joe shared a surprised look.

"I can't fathom his motives entirely. Close-lipped, he was. But we're to take a boat ride, just the two of us, today at twelve-thirty to talk things over."

"Do you suppose he's going to throw in with you?" Joe asked, with more concern evident in his voice than he desired.

"Can't say actually. The man is, as I said, close-lipped. He was the only one at yesterday's meeting I couldn't guess about. He just sat there the entire time, grinning like one of Lewis Carroll's cats. He never changed his expression, never asked a question, not a thing. Even when Farfel lunged across the table, everyone else panicked then, you know. But Caldwell, I swear he never stirred. I believe his only reaction was a bit of a chuckle."

Joe wanted to pursue Caldwell's difficult-to-determine motives further, but Karl got a question in first.

"You say you could interpret the partners' individual reactions yesterday? That fascinates me. It sounds like the

58

kind of business acumen that can't be taught, but that is either innate or learned by long experience. Are you really confident of your judgments about them?"

"Oh, quite. And I rather suppose it's innate in my case. Always could make out the other fellow's mind. Except with the rare, tough ones like Caldwell. But yesterday . . . oh, yes, it was as you Yanks say, 'a piece of cake.'"

"But the fight?" Joe asked. "Didn't that . . . well, interrupt your argument or throw off their attention or . . . something?" Joe knew he was groping.

Halsey laughed. "Yes, that. No, you see I was quite finished by then. Only the minor details left. That's why he jumped in just then. Farfel, of course. Knew he was bested, the poor chap. And I'd seen it in his eyes a half hour before. Why, he and Mrs. Bertram and the Caldwell woman were the only certain holdouts. Then there were one or two 'undecideds.' A couple of silly women who were torn between their deference to Mrs. Bertram and their greed to make a quick profit. But even those two will capitulate. Greed always betters deference."

Halsey went back to his menu, and Joe raised his eyebrows at Karl to register his disapproval of the Briton. Karl only shrugged and said, "Much as I enjoy these little talks, the golf course beckons."

"I'm anxious to get to the pool myself," Joe put in.

His colleague reacted with surprise. "The pool? You haven't taken up swimming, have you?"

"It's just for further pursuit of my spring break tan. At least I'll look like I did a lot of swimming. And I started a new novel last night that I'm eager to get back to."

The men rose and Halsey looked up to say, "Cheerio, then. I trust you'll enjoy your separate, uh, 'sports.' I know I'll enjoy mine today." Turning back to the menu, he shook his head and mumbled, "I do wish you Yanks would learn how to cook bacon properly."

"Golf?" was Joe's query once they were away from Halsey.

"Yes. The tennis courts have been a little too hot for me. Maybe I'm feeling my age, after all."

And with that they parted for the morning.

★   ★   ★

In about half an hour Joe reappeared in public, this time at the pool. He was clad in his Hawaiian print get-up, with sunglasses, tanning oil, novel, newspaper, two towels, and room key awkwardly cradled in his arms. Barely containing this load of gear, he padded around the circumference of the pool fully twice. He studied the angle of each lounge chair to the sun, estimated the same angle an hour or two hence, and considered the general view each chair provided, as well. Joe was aided in this quest by the fact that no one else had appeared at the pool at this early hour. Finally, he settled on just the right chair, one with both good sun and a good view of the pool and, in the distance, the tennis courts and golf course beyond.

Joe shed his jacket and eased back into the chair, rolling from side to side much like a small whale might wallow into a comfortable spot on the ocean floor. He leaned his head back and sighed with pleasure at the first flush of warmth from sun on his body. "Eat your hearts out, assistant professors," he mumbled. Then he took up his book to read.

Just about the same time Joe was getting settled at the pool Lord Halsey was stepping off the fifth-floor elevator in the high-rise that held his "war room." He looked up and down the hallway and, spying a maid, went to question the woman. Having been assured that, yes, she had put extra towels in the room for his wife as he'd instructed the day before, Halsey repaired to the room to work on his presentation.

The hotel was now slowly approaching its mid-morning peak of activity. The very early birds—the serious athletes like Karl who had to be up and at their sports along with the aged retirees who could never sleep late—had been at their chosen pursuits an hour or two. But now the second wave—of the vacation-lazy, the mothers with young children, and the habitual late-risers—was beginning to appear. The breakfast room was filling up as was the pool. And the raucous cries of children at play in the water—along with, one must admit, the occasional appearance of an attractive woman in a scanty swimsuit—periodically broke Joe's glued-to-the-page attention to his novel. He'd look up, frozen a moment in his "startled owl" expression. Then he'd blink, also like an owl, at the cause of his distraction, smile, and survey the beautiful vista before him before returning to his reading.

At one of those interruptions—it must have been about nine-thirty, Joe calculated later, for he had just made his second half-hour turn to ensure an all-over tan—he saw Mary Margaret Caldwell. She was dressed in a coverup and carried a beach bag. But she did not stop at the pool. Instead she circled it and went out the narrow opening in the pool's windbreak that led toward the marina. On her way to Sand Key, Joe mused, and went back to his novel.

And this was the way Joe spent his morning. He read. He turned regularly, like a slow-cooking sausage on a hand spit. He occasionally glanced up when a sound or a passing body broke his concentration. At eleven-thirty, when he'd had just enough sun by his own casual estimate, he dragged the lounge chair into a shady nook at another corner of the pool to continue reading. And had not Joe's eyes been turned at that moment he would have seen Mrs. Bertram returning to the hotel from the direction of the bay. She was red-faced, jerky in her walk, and clearly very disturbed. But Joe did not see her, and she passed the pool with not so much as a sideways glance.

Had Joe been a careful observer situated at another point on the grounds that morning he would have seen some other curious comings and goings. He would have seen, late in the morning, Helga slipping away from the Duke of Windsor suite and taking a roundabout path to her husband's office. Or he might have seen the young tennis pro, Chuck, excusing himself from the courts with a feigned excuse about an early lunch and making his own secretive way to the condominium. Or he might have seen Calvin Caldwell going to some trouble to rent a small fishing boat for a couple of hours later in the day. Caldwell had to argue strenuously to convince the hotel's boat supervisor that he would not require the services of a driver. No, he promised, he and his companion would not venture into the maze of canalways that led into the built-up areas along the bay. No, they would not go far out into the gulf, either. This transaction concluded about ten o'clock, Caldwell disappeared with the promise that he and his companion would arrive for the boat at twelve-thirty sharp.

But from his poolside vantage point Joe saw none of this activity. He did, however, as he prepared to leave for his room about twelve-forty-five, thinking eagerly of his lunch just ahead, see Mary Margaret hurrying back from Sand Key. She was alternately running and walking, and she was clearly in a hurry. She might have gone right by him, in taking a shortcut around the pool, had he not hailed the woman.

"Oh, Professor!" She was startled by his greeting.

"You look 'late for a very important date,'" Joe said with a smile.

"I beg your pardon?"

"Oh, it's just an old literary line. I meant you look in quite a hurry."

"Yes, I'm late getting back from the Cabana Club. I fell asleep on the beach. Now I've got to hurry to get cleaned up for today's business meeting." Rolling one shoulder up for his inspection, she frowned and added, "And I've got this awful sunburn. I've absolutely doused myself with lotion. But I fear I put it on too late. It didn't prevent the burn and I'm already in pain from it. I don't suppose you know any remedies?"

"Ask at the desk," Joe suggested. "They can probably recommend something."

"I suppose so," she replied distantly. The woman seemed preoccupied and clearly wanted to go on about her business. "I . . . uh," she began, not really knowing where the thought was going.

Joe took the cue and said, "Well, I've got to get ready to meet Karl for lunch myself." He began to gather up his collection of pool gear.

Mary Margaret started to leave, and Joe called after her, "Good luck in the meeting today."

"Luck?" she repeated as if puzzled. "Oh, yes," she responded, and then she hurried on to her room.

And Joe went to his room, too, quickly forgetting the exchange with Mary Margaret. His mind skipped instead to his newly acquired dislike for the game of golf. Any sport that took so long for Karl to play that it necessitated moving lunch back to one-thirty would never be one of his favorites. But then there was that old saying about half the fun in anything being in the anticipation. Joe didn't really believe that about food. Half the fun was much too high a percentage. But he was sure there was some appropriate ratio here; it was just very hard to estimate.

This last thought led Joe, as it always did, into the mental game he called "discounting your next big meal." He imagined what his lunch at one-thirty might consist of: what first course, what main course, what wine, what dessert. Next he asked himself, if I look at that future meal like the expected future return on some investment, what would be its present value to me? With the investment, I'd have to discount or reduce the dollar value of the expected return by the market rate of interest to get its present value. If the interest rate is seven percent, a dollar promised to me a year from now is worth the same as about ninety-three cents given me today. But what about that meal? Would I accept the hotel's luncheon buffet—clearly a far inferior meal—at eleven-thirty as equivalent to the full three-course lunch at one-thirty? Or would my food discount instead be such that I'd settle for two of the three full-meal courses at eleven-thirty, skip dessert, and feel satisfied in exchange for not having to wait until after one o'clock to eat? Yes, these were tough choices, Joe admitted.

Thus it was that Joe relinquished his morning's sentinel post. Not that this spot would have allowed him to see the last notable happening that morning anyway, since the pool did not overlook the back side of the condominium with Halsey's office, the side with the "super view" of the gulf. Had Joe had such a view himself, he would have been startled, as was a very late-arising young couple on their way to the boat dock, to see Lord Halsey on the sidewalk on the back side of the building. Halsey's surprised stare appeared to take in that scenic vista he'd complimented before. But in truth Halsey could not appreciate the sight—for he was quite dead. He was sprawled on the concrete, clutching a beach towel in one hand. Another towel was snagged on the limb of a water oak about ten feet or so above him. And if one took this second towel as a flag or a cue and looked still further up the building—all the way up to the fifth floor— there directly above Halsey's body was the steel railing at the balcony of his office, dangling loose and broken at one end. A third towel flapped gently in the coastal breeze from the railing.

Seven

The Candlelight Lounge at the hotel was abuzz with gossip. Joe and Karl sat nursing their drinks, saying little, and watching the flow of real and imagined information that spread from table to table. Above the murmur of cautious whispers and occasional bold assertions they could hear enough tidbits to get the flavor of what was being said.

"Some rich Briton has died in a fall from his balcony."

"A rich foreigner fell from his balcony. It looks like an accident, but . . ."

"Some foreigner may have been pushed off his balcony."

"A rich man was murdered at the hotel today."

Joe was particularly amused by all this talk. "I wonder," he said to his friend, "what will happen when two of these separate rumors, each moving around the room in a different direction, bump up against each other. I can see it now. One person will say to another at the next table: Did you hear about the foreigner who died today? They think he was murdered. And the second person will say: My word, no. And I've just learned of the publishing magnate who was definitely murdered. There must be a madman on the loose."

Karl was not amused. Gossip—unless it was about the foibles of his dean or one of his departmental colleagues—seldom interested him. And even when he was interested, he always managed to pretend that such silliness was too petty for his attention. In the present instance he was, in fact, at least mildly intrigued by Halsey's death. But he still had his usual disdain for the reaction of the crowd, as he would have put it.

Karl surveyed the room and its whispering, tittering, and arguing occupants. Then he sniffed, a bit aristocratically as if to draw himself up above all this, and said, "It's a wonder the hotel doesn't stage a death every week. The entertainment value's enormous."

"Yes, I see," Joe mused. "From that point of view it could be seen much like a good with significant commercial value. Something that could be regularly produced for its retail value."

"That's it. Death on demand," Karl agreed. "It would certainly keep the mob happy."

"Sort of 'bread and circuses,' is that it?" Joe asked, hoping Karl would catch the sarcasm.

But his companion took the remark seriously and replied, "Indeed."

Joe might have felt a touch defensive or, alternatively, abused himself in this exchange, for he was as engrossed by Halsey's death as anyone in the bar. But because of Karl's feigned lack of interest, his own gossipy thoughts, which he would have dignified by referring to as hypotheses, had to remain largely in his head. Yet Joe couldn't contain himself entirely, and every now and then an idea would bubble to the surface and he'd have to voice it.

"I wonder if he had a bad heart. Or maybe a bad heart and something like vertigo along with it, which, in combination, might have caused his fall," Joe speculated in one of these effusive moments. He was thinking now about one of his accidental-death hypotheses.

"If you were a golfer, Joe," Karl responded, "you'd have been able to press all your questions directly on the police." Karl was thinking about how, when returning from his golf game, he had seen the ambulance, the sheriff's cars, and the growing throng of curious onlookers converging on the high-rise where, unknown to him at that moment, Halsey's body had been found. Karl was sufficiently curious to wish to know the reason for this activity, so he'd joined the throng.

To his discomfort, Karl had been caught in the elbowing, shoving crowd, but he had—by virtue of his height and a little of his own shoving—gotten close enough to the cordoned-off section of the sidewalk to see a sheet-draped body and to hear Halsey's name repeated by those at the front of the throng. The balcony railing had provided him enough additional information about what might have happened so that, once having seen that, he decided to return to the hotel. Joe, of course, upon hearing this much had besieged his friend with a dozen or more questions. Could he describe the scene? Were there any witnesses? Was it thought to be an accident or . . . or something else?

Karl had protested that he didn't know any of these details. After all, why should he concern himself with such matters? And wouldn't it all be explained in ever-so-much and ever-so-gripping detail on the local TV news anyway?

But the TV news had proven uncharacteristically vague, only providing the barest of the facts about the death. So Joe was left to his questions and Karl to his guise of indifference in the bar that evening.

By this point their conversation had flagged. Joe went back to his hypotheses, and Karl fell to calculating whether he wanted another martini now that the happy hour had passed. Had his first one, he pondered, reduced the marginal utility of a second so much that the now-doubled price of another drink would be far too high? Or had, as it sometimes did, that first martini actually whetted his taste for another, *increasing* the marginal utility of a second one instead? Karl knew the latter possibility, when it occurred, was of a special class that seemed to defy the Law of Diminishing Marginal Utility. But he also knew that, in the latter situation, a second martini would satisfy all his remaining desire for alcohol for the evening.

Lost in the intricacies of these separate mental exercises, the two professors looked out of place in the bar. Where everyone else was talking or laughing, they had fallen into their separate, silent reveries. And perhaps it was this fact that caused Calvin Caldwell to stop at their table as he marched into the bar with a subdued Aaron Farfel in tow.

"Well, professors," the Texan greeted them. "Why so glum? You're not mourning the death of our British rival, are you?"

"Oh, hello, Cal," Joe responded in surprise, jarred loose from the mental labyrinth of a particularly intricate speculation about the cause of Halsey's death.

"One seldom wishes ill-will on his fellow men," Karl offered dryly, "but 'glum' is entirely too strong a description of my response to Lord Halsey's unfortunate demise."

Calvin had to repeat that last remark in his head, and then he laughed heartily and said, "That's terrific, Doc. You professors could probably be long-winded about a change in the weather."

In response to this, though largely to himself, Karl muttered, "Even as an amateur observer I recognize that meteorological dynamics are complex, necessitating detailed analysis merely for description, much less explanation."

Joe, for his part, chose to be daring and ventured the remark, "You appear not to be mourning the death yourself."

Caldwell snorted derisively, even before Karl could get out his own, faintly acid, "Or is it that you're here to drink a farewell toast to the man? I believe it fair to say that he was your kind of businessman."

"Damned tough bird, he was. That's true," Calvin agreed. "But he's dead, too, isn't he? And in business that's all that matters. No Halsey, no buy-out offer. So we the living must press on . . . right, Farfel?"

This last question came out with considerable extra emphasis, as if demanding assent from a previously wavering subject. Farfel had, in fact, looked both depressed and subdued from his arrival. He'd only nodded weakly in greeting the two professors, and then he'd hung back behind the

Texan. To the latter man's question, he only managed a grim, "Yeah, sure."

Calvin then said, "*You two* can have a drink in honor of the late Lord Halsey, while we attend to the business of the living." With that remark he nodded a goodbye and led his companion to a secluded corner table.

"Now *that's* certainly an odd couple!" Joe said with some excitement.

"Yes, I expected they'd stimulate your 'gossip glands' even further." But despite his tone, Karl was himself surprised. He added, "They do seem an unlikely pair to be engaged in a business discussion. Especially at just this moment."

"I wonder . . . ," Joe mused.

But his colleague turned a hard look on Birnoff to caution, "Now don't go cooking up any conspiracy theories about Halsey's death because of this. And especially not out loud. There's no telling what rumor you might start in this crowd. Or, for that matter, who might be listening and might get us embroiled in the whole affair."

As if on cue for this last remark, a man approached their table. Joe thought he'd seen the man before, but the unremarkable blue suit and the resolutely blank countenance evoked no recall of just where or when.

"Excuse me, Professors Teasdale and Birnoff?" the man asked quietly.

They nodded, and he continued, "I'm the hotel security officer."

Joe knew then why he could not place the man exactly. It was surely a part of his job to observe but to remain unobserved, to be an unremarkable fixture at the hotel.

"I wonder if I could impose on you for just a few minutes," the man continued. "You see, we're attempting to get statements," and here the man's already low voice dropped even lower, "from everyone who saw Lord Halsey at any time today. I believe you breakfasted with him?"

Again they nodded.

The security man rose up from his conspiratorial stoop, presumably to avoid attracting any further attention, and then he added, "I wonder if you could join me in the Belleair Room so we could get statements from you. I apologize for the inconvenience, but it's strictly routine procedure and won't take very long."

Now the man smiled and added, as if saying goodbye to old acquaintances, "I'll see you there then. I'll be along in a moment. Oh, and don't worry about your tab here. I'll get it."

The two men hesitated a second, but then they rose and departed. Had they lingered a moment at the door, they would have seen the security man making the same request of Calvin Caldwell.

There was a modest little group already assembled in the Belleair Room. In one corner a waiter from breakfast—the one who'd served Karl and Joe and Halsey—sat with the maid from the condominium. These two, alone, were enjoying themselves and the opportunity to participate in so juicy an affair. Mrs. Bertram sat, ramrod-straight and seemingly indifferent to everyone else, in a chair in the front of the room. One of the hotel's management people paced nervously in the back. Joe and Karl, upon entering, took seats near to, but respectfully distant from, Mrs. Bertram. And Joe raised an eyebrow at his colleague when a red-faced Calvin Caldwell huffed into the room shortly after them. The man folded his arms defiantly and leaned against a side wall, making it clear he was not letting his guard down even for an instant.

For a few minutes they sat—or stood—in silence. Even the hotel manager had stopped pacing, waiting expectantly for something to happen. At last the door opened and a huge black man in uniform entered, trailed by a younger, and smaller, pair of similarly attired white officers and the hotel security man.

Joe blinked at the black officer. This was probably the biggest man of any race the professor had ever seen. The man was somewhere in the upper six-foot range, literally the stratosphere for the short Birnoff. And the officer was powerfully built, with no trace of fat to mar the solid muscle that filled out his huge frame. The only incongruous element about the man was produced by the Ben Franklin glasses he wore. The glasses appeared far too small for the man's huge head, their tiny disks and thin frames looking like a portion of an ill-fitting party disguise.

Karl, unlike his colleague, was not in the least surprised by the officer's size. He had, after all, taught many years at a university where many such "pituitary cases," as one of his colleagues called them, were aggressively recruited for the football and basketball teams. Oberlin College, on the other hand, prided itself on recruiting an altogether different kind of talent, thus explaining Joe's lack of exposure to such men.

The appearance of an honest-to-God policeman after the nervous wait produced an equally nervous reaction in the group. People straightened up in their chairs. The hotel manager rose from a slouch against the wall, and Caldwell shifted his position to bring his crossed arms higher—and more defiantly—across his chest.

The officer looked around the room, perhaps counting heads or comparing the actual appearances of individuals with the descriptions he'd been given earlier. After letting them worry a bit longer about just what it was he was thinking, he said, in a surprisingly soft voice, "Good evening, I'm Detective Parker of the Pinellas County Sheriff's Department. Mr. Halsey's death occurred in our jurisdiction, and I've taken charge of the investigation. I've asked you here because it's my understanding that all of you either saw or had appointments to see Mr. Halsey today. The appointments were listed on his calendar.

"I'm asking that you provide us with written statements—Deputy Blake here has the forms—regarding the time you saw Mr. Halsey, the circumstances of your meeting, his manner, and whatever subjects you discussed with him. If you did not get to your appointment with him, I'd

71

like to know why and where you were at the appointed time."

After another of his careful pauses, the detective added, "It's all routine procedure. We just want to get some facts in order." Then, as an afterthought, he said, "Oh, yes. If you can think of anything else you've seen or heard in the last few days that might be related to Mr. Halsey's death, I'd like you to make a note of that, too."

This last remark affected everyone in the room, for they all sensed its obvious meaning. It was Mrs. Bertram, however, who asked the equally obvious follow-up question, "But . . . are we not to suppose that he . . . that he fell or perhaps slipped?"

The detective wrinkled his brow and stared back at her, seemingly considering his reply. Then, choosing his words carefully, he said, "Mrs. Bertram, isn't it? Yes, it could have been an accident. Or, for that matter, suicide. But you see—" here he stopped to look around the room before continuing, "there were signs of foul play. We must assume it was murder."

*　*　*

"Murder!" Joe exclaimed. He was so excited he was practically gobbling down his sherried oxtail soup with little regard for its taste. He and Karl were discussing, over dinner, their session with the sheriff's detective.

"Indeed," Karl replied with his customary calm. "Something to tell the folks back home, eh?"

"It's the most plausible explanation anyway," Joe continued, as much to himself as to Karl. "I'd been over all of them in my mind: heart attack or other health problem? That was possible, of course. But he wasn't *so* old and he appeared in vigorous health. *And* the joint probability of having a heart attack—or something—just at the moment when he would pitch over the balcony, well . . . that had to make it quite unlikely. Suicide? That too seemed unlikely given his frame of mind that morning. The man was on the verge of triumph rather than defeat. Accidental death? Well, now, if he were younger, the odds of that would actually be reasonable. I learned that from my insurance man, you know. But in his age group again, no, I think it no more likely than suicide. So ... we're left with homicide." Joe beamed with satisfaction at having anticipated this conclusion.

Karl was not impressed. "So you guessed the right cause of death. That hardly seems what's most important in the case of murder, now does it?"

"Ah, you mean we really should be trying to decide the 'who dun it' part! Now that seems much more difficult to explain," Joe replied.

"Oh, really! I supposed it not so very taxing."

Joe cocked an eye and studied his friend intently a second. Then he leaned closer to Teasdale, looked quickly from side to side to see if anyone at a nearby table might be listening, and asked in a whisper, "Do you think you know?"

Karl waved his hand in the air and replied, "Well, not specifically. But I think the problem could be easily solved if one simply applied the scientific method to it. The motive's obvious. It surely had to be an economic one arising out of the threat of this attempt to take over the magazine. I believe, therefore, that one should take that as his first assumption, indicating, of course, a specific kind of rational intent. Second, one should adopt a second assumption based on my long-held view that so heinous a crime is usually committed by a person somehow deficient in moral character. I suppose one could call that an assumption about individual propensity to commit criminal acts. And then ... well, then I believe one would have sufficient assumptions. Then it would simply be a matter of gathering a little data on the probable suspects. Their alibis first, of course. A few would presumably be eliminated because of good alibis. And then one ought to be able to discover the perpetrator from among the remainder by evaluating each one in terms of my two assumptions, economic motive and personal character."

It was Karl's turn to smile in self-satisfaction.

"I see," Joe said slowly, turning the explanation over in his mind. "Something of an economic model to account for the crime."

"Indeed."

"I suppose I shouldn't be surprised by your approach. It is your customary one to any behavioral problem."

Now it was Karl's turn to cast a questioning glance back at Birnoff. "And am I to infer you would approach the problem differently?" Karl asked. "In a more catholic and inductive fashion, do I gather, as well?"

"It *is* every bit as scientific," Joe said defensively. "Besides, I am not myself as confident of the suitability of any particular set of initial assumptions about the motive. That may sound naive, since the one you mention does appear quite obvious. But we know, as social scientists, that human behavior can arise for reasons rather different from the obvious. Thus I'd be disposed to avoid any initial assumptions that might restrict one's field of inquiry. I think one would wish to keep in mind several alternative possible explanations. Then he could eventually confront each of those with the objective data arising from the facts of the crime, the alibis of the suspects, their individual motives, and so on."

"I suppose one could go about it in that fashion," Karl agreed with an air of disdain, "if he had no confidence in his theory."

"It's not theory *per se*, but it's *your* theory I find uncompelling," Joe replied much as if he were thinking out loud.

"I'd wager that when the murderer's apprehended, my little model will be shown to have been entirely accurate."

"How much?" Joe demanded with a twinkle in his eye.

"Oh, I'd put up ten of my shares of that Apple Computer stock we both bought last year."

"It's a bet," Joe agreed.

74

Eight

Karl Teasdale's nose kept turning further up, or at least that was the way it appeared to his friend Joe. They had arrived at the breakfast room a little later than usual this morning, and a number of tables were already occupied. And most of the occupants were engrossed in a discussion of Halsey's death. A newly arrived couple was hearing at least three different versions of that event from people at other tables around them. But each different story was an "I swear it's true, I heard it from someone who saw or knew or talked to . . ." version.

When Karl first caught part of this conversation, he sniffed. But at least he then went back to his corn flakes. Then he heard a remark about the death from another table, and his nostrils flared. The next time he heard something, and from a third part of the room, as well, Karl raised his head as if detecting a bad odor. He glanced at the offending party and then raised himself up to his full height.

"I do believe," Karl began to say, speaking slowly and carefully to underscore the disdain he felt for those about them, "that the climate at this hotel is becoming intolerable. I fear that, were I to attempt a game of tennis this morning, I would be subjected, between volleys, to a barrage of unfounded speculation concerning this crime from the players on either court beside me."

Joe Birnoff, in spite of appearing inattentive to the world around him, was sufficiently observant of Karl's mannerisms to have seen this coming. He also knew his best course was to remain silent in the hope that Karl's anger would exhaust itself.

But Karl could become quite offended by the petty behavior of what he only rarely would admit to calling the common people. After all, it was a luxury of the isolated life of a scholar that Karl could usually avoid such people altogether. Thus his distaste for "common people's behavior," along with his limited experience with it, left him highly intolerant.

"I do not suppose there is another hotel in the area that is equivalent to this one in its amenities?" he asked after another look around the room.

"Now, Karl!"

"Do not 'now, Karl' me. You know I prefer a quiet and restful setting when we take these vacations. And you know, as well, what I think of rude and ill-behaved people."

"I understand that you're upset by all this gossip. I'm not so pleased by it myself. But it is inevitable human behavior. Besides, there's a humorous and, for that matter, an intellectually interesting side to it, if you look at it as a social scientist."

Karl rolled his eyes. "Don't tell me you're turning sociologist on me? Next you'll start talking about 'patterns of informal communication,' 'the consequences of rumor for the quality of information flow,' or maybe something like 'rumor as social myth.'"

"So you do know how to look at it like a social scientist!"

"Like a sociologist, I said. We have those flaky birds at Wisconsin, too, you know."

"Nonetheless, I don't believe we need do anything as radical as change hotels. Why don't we rent a car and begin touring the area? That'll get us out of the hotel."

"Are you certain we need to rent a car? Perhaps there are some good bus tours that are cheaper."

"You know you wouldn't like traveling with the herd on a bus tour. Besides, then we'd be forced to stick to their itinerary. I like making up my own. We'll have lots more freedom that way."

"But it always turns out to be more expensive than you say it will."

"Look at it this way," Joe offered in some exasperation. "We'll get a weekly rate and keep the car to drive ourselves back to the airport when we depart. That way we'll save taxi fare."

"That's OK if we can rent the car at the airport in the first place. Then we can avoid any drop-off charge." Having said this, however, Karl saw the flaw in his own argument. "But we'd have to pay a fare to get to the airport in the first place."

"Oh, don't be so cheap. You know we'll be happier in our own car. We'll take the hotel limo to the airport to get the car so we can drive ourselves back there when we leave. Look at it this way, maybe when we drive around you'll see some real estate you'd want to invest in next year. Then you can probably figure out some way to write the expense of the car off your income tax. As part of the cost of the investment or something. After all, you are the tax whiz."

"We bought resort property three years ago," Karl sniffed. "But I suppose it wouldn't hurt to consider what's available here."

Joe beamed with satisfaction. He knew the way to divert Karl's mind was to get onto the subject of investments.

* * *

Karl was shaking his head as the two men sought out their car in the rental agency parking lot. At first, Joe thought it was over the fact that he'd insisted on a full-sized model instead of a compact, but it turned out to be something different.

"Did you hear what that clerk said?" Karl asked with a touch of exasperation.

Joe thought a moment, but nothing remarkable came to him, so he only shook his head.

Without waiting for his companion's reaction, Karl went on, "Unlimited *free* mileage. I do wish people would be more circumspect about the use of that word."

"What word?"

"Free! Free! The mileage is not free."

"Oh, she's only a clerk. She's probably never had a course in economics."

"Nonetheless, the truth of the matter ought to be obvious, even to a simple clerk," Karl observed. "A certain amount of mileage is assumed in the determination of the rates. As a consequence, light users pay too much and heavy users pay too little. It's just another example of the nonuser paying for the user."

"We'll be sure to put a lot of miles on our car," Joe suggested.

But Karl only frowned in response. "It's the principle of the thing, you know," he shot back at his friend. But then, something else diverted Karl's attention from this subject. "Uh, Joe," he began cautiously, "are you certain you want to drive? You recall, I'm sure, what happened when we were vacationing in the Bahamas."

"I don't care what the policeman said, I still contend there was no one-way sign where we turned onto that street."

"But, nonetheless—"

Karl's protest was too late, however, for Joe quickly unlocked the car and got in the driver's seat. Then he said, "Besides, I spent a good hour last night studying a map of the area. You wouldn't know where we're going."

Karl was still uneasy and, as they drove out of the lot, he said, "I could drive and you could navigate. That might work even better if you know the route so well." This proposal got no response at all from Birnoff, but then, a few moments later, something caught Karl's eye that made him even more concerned about his friend's driving. "Joe," he asked, "are you sure you even know how to get out of the airport?"

"It's quite simple. There's only one way in and out. And the road just circles the terminal."

"That explains why we just passed the rental car agency again."

"Oh, that. I was just testing your sense of direction," Joe laughed. Then, after a darting glance from side to side, he sped off at the next turning which, fortuitously, proved to be the exit from the airport.

Some time later, after what Karl judged a surprisingly small number of false turns, they reached the Gulf-side beach at Clearwater. There they crossed the first bridge to the string of islands that paralleled the coast. "This ought to be particularly scenic," Joe explained. "We're now on an interconnected chain of islands that runs along the coast for perhaps twenty miles or so. Sand Key, the island with the hotel's cabana club, is part of this chain. I thought we'd drive south down these islands toward St. Petersburg to get a view of the major resort areas. Then we can take another bridge back over to the mainland—at any of several points. I marked a couple of local restaurants on the map. We'll probably be in the area of one or another of them in time for lunch."

"I suppose it's pleasant enough," Karl agreed. "But all these scenic views begin to look alike to me after a while. Besides, I thought we might want to chat a little about the next round of revisions in our text, now that we have some quiet time together."

Joe was suspicious. "I thought we were both pretty happy with the way things stood after the last revisions. Except for the inevitable need to bring a few statistics up to date here and there, and maybe to keep our economic policy chapters current."

"That's just what I had in mind. I thought we ought to expand our macroeconomic material a bit."

"I thought we had finally reached agreement on that. You recall how our editor loved my new introduction: that discussion about the responsibility of contemporary government, in

79

the area of the 'positive state' or simply of 'big government,' if you want to use the more pejorative term, to ensure steady economic growth and ameliorate recessions. After that, it seems to me we treat the alternative policy approaches to that goal quite fairly. There's certainly as much monetarism in there as I can tolerate, and I know you feel the same way about the Keynesian material. Or, as we agreed to call it, the post-Keynesian material. And, if I can toot my own horn, I especially like my new, expanded discussion of how, under the Keynesian approach, the manipulation of governmental fiscal policy can impact aggregate demand and hence the GNP. You must admit that I developed some terrific new examples in that section."

"Watch out for that kid on his bicycle," Karl warned. "Maybe I shouldn't have raised this topic when you're driving, but . . . well, what you just said is precisely the problem. It's precisely because you expanded the Keynesian explanation so much that I think we need to do the same with the supply-side economics material."

"It seems sufficient to me."

"Who's surprised," Karl reacted. "You Keynesians—and let's just drop the *post-* or *neo-* or whatever qualifiers you'd like to use to show how you've all actually gone beyond old John Maynard when in reality you haven't—you Keynesians only want to talk about the effects of fiscal policy on demand and on GNP. You always ignore the effects on supply."

"And why should you care? You monetarists and your camp-following supply-siders and rational expectationists don't think fiscal policy has any long-term effect anyway. Just as long as you could keep your precious supply of money growing at a stable rate. If only macroeconomic policy could be just that simple!"

"Say, are you about to turn here?" Karl had suddenly realized that his friend had, in his typically last-second fashion, decided to move into the left turn lane at a traffic light.

"I thought we'd cross back to the mainland here at Belleair Causeway. It's a short-cut back to the hotel."

"But that sign we just passed said this'll be a toll bridge. Aren't there any free ones?"

Joe frowned and said, "Yes, but they're further along, well past the hotel."

"Skip the short-cut. We can take in a little more of this quote-free-unquote drive you were touting, and then we'll take a free bridge, as well. And don't complain. After all, I didn't when you rented this big car rather than a compact."

"Oh, *touché*," Joe conceded. Then he awkwardly worked his way out of the left turn lane, to the consternation of the other drivers around him.

"Now where was I," Karl wondered out loud. "Oh, yes, I'm amazed that you poor Keynesians don't feel lonely these days, given the number of both academic and governmental camp-followers, as you put it, that have been convinced by our monetarist arguments about appropriate stabilization policy."

"Wrong-headedness is still wrong-headedness, regardless of whether it's preached by one or a hundred," Joe replied.

"So you'd deny that the frequent manipulation of fiscal policy to attempt, and I emphasize the word *attempt*, to achieve stabilization by the Keynesian approach—and I'll set aside for the moment the question of whether public officials even have the strength of will to ignore their other spending and taxing objectives to concentrate on stabilization goals— you'd deny that such manipulation creates tax incentives that have devastating effects on production over the long term?"

Joe frowned and said, "The beneficial effects of fiscal policy on aggregate demand far outweigh any possible adverse incentives of the taxes, if there are any in the first place."

Now it was Karl's turn to react. He threw up his hands and blew out a big breath of air in mock disgust. "Oh, my. You Keynesians have always taught your students that an extra dollar spent by the government—whether from borrowing or taxing—increases GNP. But can't you see this instruction has ignored the fact that government expenditures crowd out private ones?"

"But part of the tax that is ultimately collected to pay for these expenditures comes from what people would have saved."

"And what others would have invested!" Karl responded with increasing exasperation.

"You must admit, going back to your own argument a moment ago about how many people are in your camp today, that Keynesian policy has had a lot of supporters for quite a long time."

"And who's surprised? It offered a perfect rationale for every politician with a pet spending project. Each one could claim that his project would help raise the GNP and thus would help the entire nation, not just his state or district."

"But you forget the reverse side of Keynesian policy, the dampening effect it has on too-rapid growth during periods of inflation."

"Ha! And why is it that to achieve that dampening we always had to have a tax increase instead of a spending decrease?"

Joe shrugged as if the answer were obvious. "It's simply easier to change taxes than to alter government programs in midstream." Then he added, "Oh, by the way, there's a sign for a free bridge. I'm going to turn here. Now there's no telling where we'll have to eat lunch."

"You and your stomach! But you're not getting away with changing the subject to food. Easier to change taxes, my foot! Let's be more precise. What you mean is that it's politically easier. All those politicans are afraid to cut the pork-barrel spending that they think is so crucial to getting re-elected."

"But the object, after all, is to fight short-term cyclical swings. Does it really matter which mechanism you use?"

"I think we're back to my point about the crowding-out effect," Karl said.

"Your hypothesis," Joe corrected. "I've yet to see a fair empirical demonstration of those effects."

"Well, you certainly can't deny that politicians mostly ignore the long run for the apparent short-term 'quick fix.'

And I emphasize the apparent character of those short-run solutions, since their proponents inevitably ignore the adverse long-run consequences."

Now Joe was getting equally excited. "Those long-run supply-side effects are way overblown. Like I just said, there's no evidence that past tax policy has had those disincentive effects."

"What about the Laffer Curve point that increasing tax rates, once you're over the hump of the curve, actually will decrease tax revenues because of the effect on incentives?"

"Oh, yes. The famous curve first drawn on a paper napkin. It's certainly worth the paper it was written on."

"That's not fair. You know—"

"That there's no evidence that the nation was over the hump of the Laffer Curve in its tax policy."

"And why is it, then," Karl demanded, "that after the Reagan tax cuts the revenues collected from higher-tax-bracket individuals rose instead of fell?"

Seemingly in response to this question, Joe jerked his head in surprise. But then he said, "Speaking of rising, isn't this bridge a bit steep?"

"And what are those bells and sirens for? Joe, watch out!"

* * *

The receptionist at the Biltmore was smiling and shaking her head as she returned from her coffee break. Seeing another clerk behind the desk, she laughed and said, "Tommie, I've just heard the funniest story on the radio. It seems these two college professors were out for a drive on the beaches. They were having a big argument, and they got so caught up in it they weren't watching where they were going."

"So, did they drive into the surf, or what?" the impatient Tommie asked.

"No, it was worse—or better, actually—than that. They'd turned at Madeira Beach to cross the bridge back to the mainland. But the driver was so engrossed in the argument that he ignored the red light and the fact that the drawbridge had started to go up. They drove right under the barricade as it was coming down. Then the front wheels of the car went over the edge of the bridge and they were stuck there."

"Amazing!" Tommie agreed.

"Yeah. And they were balanced so precariously that the bridge tender was afraid to lower the bridge. He had to call the fire department, and they had to break out the car's back window and take the professors out on a fire ladder."

"Maybe there should be a law," Tommie laughed, "that these intellectual types should have to stick to bicycles."

Not long after this conversation Karl and Joe arrived back at the hotel—in a taxi. The two men, grimly silent, looking a bit tattered and tousled, and evidently a bit angry at each other, collected their keys and started for their rooms. But they were accosted by a bellboy who had been searching the hotel for them for most of the afternoon.

"Oh, Professor Teasdale. Professor Birnoff," the young man hailed from behind them.

But when the two men turned in response, the bellboy was taken aback by their disheveled attire and their near-angry stares. "Wha . . . what happened?" he stammered.

"We've been having an argument," Karl replied archly, as if the explanation for their appearance should be obvious.

"A discussion," Joe corrected.

"Er . . . who won?" the boy asked.

Joe cast a sheepish glance at his friend and said, "I suppose you could say we reached a draw. Now, what was it you wanted?"

"Oh, right. That Detective Parker from the Sheriff's Department. He wants to see you both."

Nine

The bellboy led the two professors into the private maze of offices that housed the hotel's management staff. There, in a small, ill-lit and ill-furnished back corner cubicle, they found Detective Parker. The man was sitting bolt upright at the one desk, his arms crossed rigidly over his chest. He was staring at a small blackboard covered with messy writing.

The bellboy announced their arrival and then departed so quickly Joe suspected he'd been chastised on other occasions for lingering to overhear the proceedings. The two professors went into the room and nodded at the detective.

At first they weren't certain he knew they were there. True enough, he did turn to look at them. But he only turned his head; his body remained squared toward the blackboard across the room. And his hard expression didn't change at all.

The two professors shifted uncomfortably and, while Joe blinked at the policeman, Karl asked, "Er, you sent for us?"

The officer answered Karl's question with only his hard stare for perhaps ten seconds before saying, "Yeah." Then the man uncrossed his arms and got up from his chair, rising to his full height to tower over both Joe and Karl. And Parker's imposing stature accelerated the rate of Joe Birnoff's nervous, rapid-fire blinking.

"Sit here," he directed, pointing to two plain chairs before the desk. The man's tone, Karl noticed, was considerably harder-edged than it had been the evening before in the Belleair Room.

They sat down and the policeman looked from one to the other and asked, pointing first at Karl and then at Joe, "Teasdale, right? And Birnoff?"

They nodded.

"Professors, right?"

Again they nodded.

"And staying how long at the hotel?"

There was a little pause of uncertainty before Joe answered, "We're here for two weeks."

"Two weeks!" Parker shot back. "Pretty expensive place for two weeks. I never knew any college professors that could afford a vacation like that."

The statement seemed to demand a reply, and Karl so bristled at the man's tone and insinuation that he answered, "Neither Professor Birnoff nor I is your average college professor. We are full professors by rank at our respective universities, and we are highly successful and distinguished members of our particular academic discipline."

Joe Birnoff started blinking again, but this time it was in response to Karl's assessment of just who they were. Gee, I suppose he's right, Joe thought. Who'd have ever imagined he'd say such things about a Keynesian!

But Joe didn't let his mind drift far, for he had his own response to the policeman. "Yes, you see it's just our even-year, royalty income vacation."

It was the policeman's turn to react in surprise and then ask, "Your what?"

Joe explained with some noticeable pride. "Professor Teasdale here, Karl, and I wrote some years ago an economics textbook which has enjoyed, shall we say, continuing modest success over the years. So each year in February we both receive from our publisher a check for royalty income for the past year's sales."

After a quick smile at Karl, Joe continued, "After our very first successful year, when we were both glowing over

86

that first royalty check, I convinced Karl that we ought to celebrate. I got him to agree to spend part of the income on a spring vacation somewhere where we could get away from the winter weather."

"And I accepted the suggestion," Karl put in, "on the condition that the following year we invest an equivalent amount of our next royalty check in some long-term investment."

"So there it is," Joe concluded. "The pattern became quickly institutionalized, dare I use that academic word. In even-numbered years we take a spring vacation. And in odd-numbered years we invest. I plan the vacations, and Karl plans the investments."

Parker thought about this explanation a moment, toying absentmindedly with a pencil on his desk. Then he looked up and shook the pencil at them as he asked, "So you have no connection with this bunch of, what is it, Arsgratia people?"

"We have no business association with them," Karl responded. "We have had occasion—largely on the basis of chance encounters—to meet and become acquainted with some of the principals in that enterprise."

"Farfel?" the officer demanded.

"Yes."

"Bertram, the old lady?"

"Yes."

"Caldwell, Mr. or Mrs.?"

"Both," Karl replied with some satisfaction.

Parker, in response, raised his eyebrows before asking, "What about Halsey himself?"

"Yes, we met him as well."

"Well, what about his wife, that . . . that Helga woman?"

"We met her briefly in the bar. And I had a tennis game with her."

Now Parker crossed his arms again and said, "That's a hell of a lot of chance encounters."

"It is a small hotel," Joe offered with a touch of meekness. And, largely to himself, he added, "I could calculate the probabilities for you, if you wish."

"I believe it fair to say," Karl added, "that we became somewhat popular with several of those people. You know, of course, of Halsey's purpose here. Well, when some of the partners learned our profession, they quite naturally sought our advice on this takeover effort. All on a strictly informal basis, of course."

"Of course," the detective repeated.

Karl didn't like the man's tone, but he ignored it to go on, "Why even Halsey had occasion to discuss the matter with us."

"And his wife, what did she have occasion to discuss with you? I know she's into some physical sports besides tennis."

Karl rocked back in his chair, stung by the insinuation. But he mastered his initial outrage sufficiently to reply, "I believe you are aware that we, Professor Birnoff and I, observed some of the woman's promiscuous behavior. I noted that in the statement I gave yesterday. As to my own relations with her, they consisted, as I've already stated, of one meeting in the bar—with both Halsey and Professor Birnoff present—and then one game of tennis. I am not, Detective Parker, in the habit of responding to the unsolicited invitations of oversexed women of any age, nationality, or character. And I suspect that you have far richer fields to plow in order to solve this crime."

Karl's anger and bluntness apparently checked Parker. The detective eased back in his chair and seemed to shrink a bit in weariness. "All right, all right," he replied. "I just have to probe these things."

The officer shook his head, and then he rose to pace the room. He *was* tired. They could see it in the slump of his shoulders, and they could hear it in the changed tone of his voice as he asked, now with something like weary hope instead of the earlier blunt forcefulness, "Tell me something else then. How come you two are so . . . so *certain* about things?"

"I beg your pardon?" Karl was still suspicious, wondering if this was simply a different approach to entrapping them.

"Yeah, let me show you." Parker took up a folder of papers from the desk and began to rifle through it. He paused occasionally, reading a few lines to himself, and then went on to another page in the file. "I want a particularly good one," he explained, "although they're really all about the same."

Finally he took a page from the folder and said, "Ah, yes. This one's the best." He scanned the page a moment and then began to read aloud, "I slept late—maybe until nine or ten." Parker stopped, looked up at them and added, "First he wrote ten, then he marked that out and put nine. Then he marked that out and put 'nine or ten.'" Parker shook his head and went back to reading from the page, "Then I lay about the room reading magazines until time for lunch. I suppose I went down to eat about noon, that's when I usually eat. At the dining room I met—" here Parker waved his hand and verbally inserted the word "blank" for the actual name. Then he read on, "I don't know whether 'blank' was about to enter or leave the dining room, but she wanted to talk, so we went to the bar and discussed the upcoming business meeting for perhaps an hour. I probably stopped by the newsstand next to get a copy of the *Times*. It never comes before lunch. Then, when I arrived at the business meeting, maybe about two-fifteen, I was informed of Halsey's death."

The policeman looked up at them again and asked, "Well, what do you think?"

The two professors looked at each other and then back at Parker.

"Is there some hidden clue in the passage?" Joe ventured.

"You don't get it? Then let me read an entirely different one." This time Parker flipped open the file and took a page off the top of the stack. He read down a few lines, mouthing the words to himself, until he said, "Now try this in comparison." He quoted, "I rose at seven sharp, just in time to catch the morning news on the radio. It was the CBS radio news on the local affiliate station. The lead story was about the economy. The Consumer Price Index was reported to have fallen three-tenths of a percent last month. Not that I was surprised myself, having known about the prior month's—" Here Parker waved his hand and said "blah,

blah, blah." Then he continued to read, "After a quick shower I met—" again Parker inserted "blank" and then read on, "for breakfast at seven-thirty. We met 'blank' upon entering the dining room and joined her at her table. Ordinarily, I have only coffee and toast, but I knew lunch would be late that day, so I had oatmeal with fruit, as well. 'Blank' left before we were ourselves finished, shortly before eight o'clock, and 'blank' came in after her. He joined us and we talked of—" Here Parker said again in summary, "blah, blah, blah." Then he skipped down the page to read, "Before nine o'clock I was at the pool to get some sun. 'Blah, blah, blah.' At twelve-forty-five I met 'blank.'"

Parker stopped reading and looked up at the two professors. Joe was smiling broadly and Karl, by now, had surmised why.

"They're both like that," Parker said. "You two may be the only people in this hotel who can remember what you had for dinner three days ago—and just how and how well it was prepared. And times! Nobody remembers times so exactly."

He paused to shake the page in his hand at the file folder. "Everybody else," he went on, "they're vague about details, inaccurate with a lot of facts, admittedly uncertain about a number of things—thank goodness for the nosiness of hotel maids to correct some of those problems—and ... well, they're just like I expect witnesses and suspects to be. But you two, you remember everything!"

"Knowledge and information are the bedrocks of our profession," Joe said with a smile. "We're trained to be careful observers, attentive to detail, and analytic in our thinking."

"And," Karl added, "my colleague here schedules the rest of his existence around the pleasures of the table. He is conscious of the passing of every hour because of its relation to his next meal."

"And *my* colleague here—" Joe tried to rebut, but Parker cut him off.

"OK, OK, I guess I've got the idea."

Parker tossed the paper down and began to pace the room. As he did so, he glanced at the blackboard but then dropped his eyes toward the floor as if composing his next thought. Then he began slowly to say, much as if he were talking to himself rather than the two professors, "OK, let's say you don't have any connection with these people beyond the ones you've mentioned. Let's say then that neither of you has any motive for which you should be considered a suspect in Halsey's death. And let's say, as well, that your unusual powers of factual recall are just, well, they're just products of your professional training. In that case I'm now especially interested in one or two things you both put in your statements."

Parker went back to his desk and took up one of the papers again. "Now, both of you mention seeing Halsey's wife with that kid, the assistant tennis pro. And it happened when you were talking to Halsey. But here's one of the few points where you're *uncertain* for a change. Did Halsey, or did he not, see the kid with his wife?"

Joe and Karl looked at each other a moment, and then Joe shrugged in indecision. He said to Parker, "We really can't say for certain. Halsey was turning back to look at us just when that boy, what's-his-name, walked onto the balcony."

"Chuck," Karl reminded him.

"Yes, Chuck," Joe agreed. But then he could only smile weakly at Parker as if to add: I'm sorry, but we just don't know.

Parker frowned. Then he looked down at the paper again and asked. "OK, how about this? Did anyone else know of Helga's promiscuous behavior?"

Again the two professors looked at each other, and this time they both shrugged.

Parker shook his head in frustration, and Karl was forced to respond, "I'm quite certain anyone remotely observant of human behavior would have noticed her surface flamboyance. Certainly, Helga acts and dresses and talks as if she's promiscuous. But that could just as well be a pose. Although Professor Birnoff and I, of course, have first-hand evidence that it's more than that. Nonetheless, she *could* be acting that way just because she thinks it's expected of her. And others might be led, by those appearances alone, to *assume* she's quite promisçuous. That would be a common assumption, I would guess, about people in her, uh, profession. After all, I believe she is well known, in the circles that know such things, as having been featured in a number of *risqué* movies. Yet regarding who, in fact, knew of her alleged infidelities ... well, Professor Birnoff and I simply can't be certain of that. We have no explicit information on that point."

This explanation disturbed more than mollified the detective, but he decided to try one more time. "Well, how about this?" he asked. "Professor Birnoff, you say that on the day of Halsey's death you spent the morning at the pool. You noted the people who you saw that morning. And with close estimates of the time at which you saw each one."

"Yes, I was trying to stay conscious of the time. Didn't want to get a sunburn, you know. And," here Joe paused to smile at Karl before adding, "I didn't want to be late for lunch."

"Yes, yes. But here in your statement you mention meeting Mrs. Caldwell who claimed she was on her way back from Sand Key. You say she was distracted and seemed disturbed about something."

"I believe I said more than that. She was disturbed, but she claimed it was because of the sunburn she'd gotten on the beach."

"What would you say if I told you she had, in fact, gone to Sand Key? And that she had returned on the hotel's launch just as she said? But that, according to the statement of the launch operator, she'd arrived back at the dock a good thirty minutes before you met her at the pool? Now, you can walk from the dock to the pool in less than five minutes. In light of those facts, wouldn't you agree that Mrs. Caldwell's disturbed behavior now becomes far more interesting? In thirty minutes she could have dropped in on Halsey, had a violent argument with him about this business deal, pushed him off the balcony in the process, and still had time to hurry back to the hotel by the time which you so exactingly noted that you met her."

Parker stopped, crossed his arms, and stared at Joe in self-satisfaction.

Karl blew out an angry breath and mumbled, "Why, I never. It's simply . . . simply preposterous to suspect that nice young woman."

But Joe, despite his renewed rapid-fire blinking, was not ruffled by this suggestion or by the blunt manner of its presentation. He flapped his arms to ease those non-existent shirt sleeves once again out of his non-existent jacket. And then his eyes seemed to twinkle in recognition of some important thought and he said, "Oh, yes. Now I understand. At first it was our relative *certainty* about factual details that you couldn't understand. Nobody remembers facts like that, you said, or something to that effect. And now it's our *reticence* about drawing conclusions about yet other matters that frustrates you. Isn't that it, Detective Parker?"

Without noticing whether he got a reply—Joe was contemplating that imaginary blackboard in the sky—the professor thought a moment and then went on. "Yes, I see now. It's becoming entirely clear. But you must understand that our reticence at this point, too, is a product of our scientific temperament and training."

"Scientific?" the detective repeated, as if the idea were an entirely new one for him.

"That's right. It's not just that we're scholars accustomed to working with lots of dusty old books and to filling our heads with mountains of trivial facts. Trivial, of course, only from the point of view of others outside our profession. That might account for our facility with and recall of factual information. But there's more to it than that."

Parker sighed, now beginning to recognize what he was in for. "Somehow, I was afraid of that," he said.

"We're trained as scientists, social scientists," Joe explained. "That means, of course, that we are quite concerned with precision about factual matters. We're trained to observe carefully and to remember precisely. But surely you intuit the obverse side of that training, as well."

Joe paused, but it was not really for a reply. He frowned and then asked rhetorically, "Or is it the 'reverse' side? Or, then, again perhaps it's simply the 'flip side,' dare I use so casual an expression."

Parker rolled his eyes at this verbal perambulation. And even Karl sighed. He could easily imagine the detective's likely conclusions about the mental character of college professors based on Joe's performance.

But Joe was oblivious to these reactions. He was still in mental "outer space," running through the rest of the argument in his head before expressing it aloud. And because Joe was so obviously preoccupied with his own thoughts, Parker was uncertain whether the professor expected a reply to his last remark. So the detective decided the best course, in spite of his confusion, was to say, "Surely," and hope it would induce the professor to complete his thoughts.

"Indeed," Joe went on at last. "Consonant with an appreciation for facts is an appreciation for uncertainty. That is to say, of course, that when a scientist *doesn't* know the facts or *cannot* know the facts or finds his facts to be incomplete or in conflict among themselves . . . well, in all such situations the scientist has an obligation to admit his uncertainty. The last thing he would want to do would be to jump to an inference as yet unsupported by appropriate empirical evidence. That would be entirely too sloppy, so to speak, now wouldn't it? One must necessarily be tentative, at best, in such situations."

Joe finally looked directly at the detective who, for his part, now looked a beaten man, one clubbed down by the blows of this wordy monologue. And Joe concluded, "Thus, you see, I'm sure, why we can offer no *certain reply* one way or the other to these last questions you raise."

Evidently, the professor's stress on the words "certain reply" signalled nothing to the detective. For the subdued man could only whisper, "Damn!"

Ten

Joe Birnoff was excited. And, as he often did when he was in this state, he was talking with considerable energy. And he was pacing—pacing in a circle, in fact, around poor Karl, who was sitting on a bench by the tennis courts, lacing his shoes for a game.

"But I gave him the perfect opening," Joe was saying. "All he had to ask was: 'What, then, would you *speculate* to be the explanation for this crime?' I was terribly disappointed."

Karl frowned and shook his head. He was thinking, Joe's followed me all the way from my room to breakfast and now to my tennis match. Next, he'll probably stand on the sidelines and shout to me between volleys. But Karl kept his temper and said, "You expect too much. I'd wager that the average policeman—just like the average person—seldom considers the distinction between hypotheses which we've yet to test, our *speculations* to use your word, and our tested and therefore either supported or rejected ones. Anyway, did you consider the possibility that Parker simply had no interest in your speculations?"

"No interest?" The idea was an entirely new one for Joe.

"Indeed. After all, you are—we are, for that matter—merely witnesses to some of the incidental and probably only secondary events leading up to this crime. Detective Parker likely has a dozen other similar witnesses to suffer through, each with his or her own clever speculations about the crime."

"But we're—" Joe did not get to finish his thought before Karl interrupted.

"Yes, yes: scientists. But I fear that's about as important to Detective Parker as it is to my auto mechanic when I take in my car with a careful recital of her latest grunts and groans—accompanied by my equally careful and entirely un-tutored speculations about their causes."

Karl surely hoped he'd ended this discussion and, at the same time, calmed Joe's nervous energy by these last re-marks. It was the case that Joe stopped his circling of the bench to consider them. Yet it turned out that Joe was still not finished either.

"But he knows we're careful observers," Joe began again. "He saw that in the statements we gave. Why, then, wouldn't he be interested, if only for, dare I say, 'academic purposes,' in our guesswork, as well?"

"*Joe,*" his friend shot back with some sternness. "There is an alternative explanation—besides his simply not caring, of course. You saw how tired the man was when we arrived. Right?"

"I suppose so," Joe admitted weakly.

"That's good, especially if you're such a careful observer. Well, my point is that he was a lot more tired by the time we left. That is, by the time you'd stopped lecturing him about the scientific method."

"You mean?"

"That's right. I'm afraid you lectured him into near-stupefaction at the end there. Probably reinforced every bias he ever had about long-winded college professors at the same time."

"Oh." Joe was truly surprised by this possibility. This time he actually slumped down onto the bench to consider the ef-fect his monologue might have had on Detective Parker.

Karl went on preparing his gear for the tennis game. His opponent, a tanned and fit-for-his-middle-age businessman from Baltimore, was already on the court doing his loosening-up exercises. When he was himself almost ready, Karl turned to his silent friend to ask, "So I take it you've calmed down about this affair? I suppose you're ready now to loaf about the pool with a good book or perhaps find a foursome for bridge?"

Joe squinted at an imagined spot before him, and then he said, not so much in reply but rather as a result of some new tack his thinking had just taken, "What would really be useful would be for us to know what Parker knows. *And* to know about *his* speculations as a result. After all, he presumably has a lot of physical evidence and the results of other people's testimony that we know nothing about."

"Joe!" Karl tried another of his stern rebuffs.

But Joe ignored him. Instead of responding, in fact, Joe rose and began to pace again, this time back and forth before the bench. His head was down and his hands were pushed deep into his huge "safari" shorts.

"We'll only learn what Parker knows," Joe was mumbling, "if we gain his confidence. And since he didn't allow us a chance at that last night—by cutting off our speculative thinking—we'll have to do it another way. I suppose we'll have to acquire some evidence of our own. Maybe then we can arrange something of a trade: our evidence for his."

"Joe!" Karl said again. But he sounded more worried than angry this time.

Joe took another turn or two in his pacing and then he looked up at his friend with a glimmer of humor in his eyes and added, "Besides, I've got those shares of Apple Computer stock on the line."

With the last remark Joe's entire demeanor had changed. He had come back to the real world from whatever distant mental place he'd been inhabiting. He looked at Karl's tennis racket—which his friend was now twirling nervously—as if he'd just seen it for the first time. And then he said, "Oh. I see you're going to play a little tennis. Good idea. I think I'll wander off for a little amusement myself."

"Uh, Joe." Now Karl was entirely worried. "Joe, just what have you got in mind?"

"In mind? Whatever do you mean?"

"You're not about to start playing amateur detective, are you, Joe?"

"Karl, your opponent's waiting. I'd best let you get on with your game. Wouldn't want to disturb your sweaty regimen."

Birnoff started to move away.

"Now, Joe, listen to me—"

"See you at lunch, Karl. Twelve sharp, right?"

With the last remark Joe hurried off, while Karl, with a touch of miffed anger showing on his wrinkled brow, could only mutter, "Damn." Karl looked down at the tennis racket in his hands and then across the court at his opponent and uttered another, somewhat louder, "Damn!"

Karl thought a moment, tapping the racket against the palm of his hand. Then he walked quickly onto the court and shouted to the businessman from Baltimore, "Shall we volley a little to warm up?"

Without waiting for an answer Karl fired a hard shot across the court. He then proceeded to return, with precise, economical strokes—the next four returns from his foe. Then, with the first shot that came to his backhand side, Karl made a long, exaggerated stretch to reach the ball. But instead of making the shot, he let out a howl from mid-stretch and dropped his racket. Then he half-rose, clutching the back of one thigh.

From this doubled-over pose, Karl called to his opponent, "It's a muscle pull. Can't go on. Sorry."

Karl then hobbled about the court—as if imitating some lame animal scratching for food—picking up his racket and loose balls. Karl Teasdale was not one to abandon a nearly new set of tennis balls just because of a little physical pain. He then limped to the courtside bench, collected his bag, and, with his assortment of gear clutched in one hand and with the other hand still grasping his thigh, he nodded a farewell to the businessman from Baltimore, mumbled

98

"Sorry" again, and hobbled off. Once out of sight of the courts, however, Karl straightened up and walked hurriedly away—with an entirely healthy gait.

*　*　*

Anyone who knew Joe Birnoff well would have recognized his frustration. It showed—or would have to the knowledgeable observer—in his manner. He was breathing a bit quickly. His eyes were set in what appeared a permanent squint. And he was mumbling periodically to himself, lamenting the lack of success at his present task. Despite his frustration, however, Joe refused to give in. He'd been to the hotel patio where breakfast was served. He'd been through the lobby and down to the boat launch, checking the pool along the way. He'd even followed a long-shot idea and looked over the tennis courts and as much of the golf fairways as a few strategic vantage points would allow. But his intended quarry was nowhere to be seen.

At this point Joe might have been about to give up. Yet he had one last idea, so he peeked inside the hotel bar and discovered Aaron Farfel sitting alone in a back corner.

Joe studied Farfel a minute from a distance, then the professor ran a hand through his hair—disheveling rather than smoothing it—and crossed the room to Farfel's table. By the time he arrived there Joe had, as well, acquired an expression of weary frustration.

"Ah, Mr. Farfel," Joe hailed. "Might I join you? I'm certainly in need of a drink."

Farfel cocked his head, which bore its own weary visage, and he waved lamely at a chair. "Why not," he said. "Join the party. We're having such great fun, me and my martini."

Farfel didn't stir out of his dejected slump, but from his still-cocked head he eyed the professor. And Joe gave him a little something to study by dropping wearily into his own chair and then passing a nervous hand over his brow. To the instantly appearing waitress, Joe mumbled "a Bloody Mary," and then he fingered the cocktail napkin she left behind.

"So what's with you, Professor?" Farfel asked.

Joe shook his head and replied, "In truth, I'm not certain." Then he looked up at Farfel with an odd expression before asking, "Would you say it's morning or afternoon, Mr. Farfel?"

Before Farfel could even grasp the question, Joe went on, "And is it day or night? And are you certain just which it is? For that matter, would you say that's a red polo shirt you're wearing? Come now, might it not be maroon or wine or burgundy instead?"

Farfel gave Joe a puzzled look, to which the professor responded by saying, "Now, come now, Mr. Farfel, are you certain that you got out of bed this morning? And did you arise from the left side or the right side? Oh, the right side! Can you prove that?"

Joe paused and shrugged at his now thoroughly confused companion. Then he said in explanation, "Detective Parker. I've just spent one of the longest hours of my life with him. It was grueling. And now I'm not entirely certain whether I'm sitting at this table this very moment. And if I thought I knew, I'd certainly not venture my opinion in front of him. He'd give you the legendary 'third degree' even over that."

Farfel responded with a short, unhappy laugh. "Yeah," he said, "I know just what you mean. The man's a shark. He put me through a very mean session, too. And if he doesn't come up with the culprit soon, I've no doubt there'll be another session. My little scuffle with Halsey—I'm sure you remember that—put me high on Parker's list of suspects."

Farfel laughed his unhappy laugh again and added, "Yeah," once more. Then, just before taking another drink, a new thought occurred to him and he asked over the rim of his glass, "So what's he want of you? You aren't a suspect too are you, Professor? Or has he got you pegged for some angle to do with *Artworld*, as well?"

Joe shook his head and, after casting a quick sideways glance to see if anyone was in earshot, he leaned over the table and whispered, "It's Mrs. Bertram. I believe he suspects Mrs. Bertram."

Farfel reacted violently. He jolted up from his slouch and almost shouted, "What? That's preposterous!" Then, realizing how loud he'd been, he looked quickly around the room and added in a quieter voice, "Ann Neal Bertram? Of the Boston Bertrams. And, for that matter, of the Philadelphia Neals. The man's insane. Why, why ... what could he be thinking?"

"I know, I know," Joe agreed. "It seems ludicrous to me, too. But it's this Arsgratia business, of course. And she stood to lose more than anybody. Along with you, I guess."

Farfel didn't react, at least openly, to the last comment. Instead, he only shook his head and replied, "Yeah, but murder? Nah, Professor, this cop's a loony if he thinks that."

"He didn't tell me his evidence and, of course, I had to surmise some things based on what little he did say. But ... I think he's serious."

"Jeez," Aaron reflected. "And I thought he was ready to pin it on me."

"Have you no alibi?"

Farfel shrugged. "I guess not really. I was in my room all morning. Just moping around. You simply cannot imagine how depressed I was by the thought of what was to happen at the business meeting that day. Why, it took all morning just to pull myself together enough to get dressed."

They stared at their drinks for almost a full minute before Farfel repeated, "Mrs. Bertram! Preposterous!" Then he went on, "Sure, the magazine meant a lot to her, but murder?"

"*Means* a lot to her, that is," Joe corrected him. "The magazine *means* a lot to her. She still has it, now that Halsey's dead."

"Oh, yeah."

That last exchange subdued Farfel again, so Joe asked, "I don't know her well, of course, but it does seem out of character for her. She seems such a, well, I guess such a good person under that patrician exterior."

"She *is* a good person," Aaron replied archly. "She cares about people. And about art. And there are fewer and fewer

101

people you can say that of these days. But she especially cares about people. I've seen her help simply tons of young artists. And she's helped me, too. Hired me for this job and saved me from the slow-death torture of being a part-time art critic, part-time gallery owner, and full-time pauper."

"So she brought you in to edit *Artworld*?"

"Yeah. And she gave me nearly total editorial control. I've built this magazine. It was my judgment about art—and her money, of course—that made our reputation."

"What about the other partners? Did they play much of a role?"

"Nah, they just gave some bucks. And provided some visibility. You know, we used their names on the masthead of the magazine to add to its prestige. But mostly, they just came to these damned partners' meetings once a year. All for a little ritual of mutual back slapping over the nobility of subsidizing the magazine—coupled with some equally ritualistic hand wringing about why art can't pay its own way without the subsidy. Most of them are even too slow-witted to see the contradiction there. If art could pay its own way, we'd have no need of them. So these meetings are a waste of time as far as I'm concerned."

"These meetings, too, were Mrs. Bertram's idea, I surmise."

"Sure, and for a third kind of ritual: the *appearance* that the partners were somehow actually involved with the magazine."

"And this hotel, this location, she chose that as well?"

Farfel shot the professor an annoyed glance, as if this question touched upon an old, tender wound. "It wasn't *my* idea, dearie. I didn't even know there *was* a west coast of Florida before we started these meetings."

Again they fell silent. Joe appeared to be thinking over their conversation. Finally, after a careful sip of his drink, he concluded, "Well, for Mrs. Bertram's sake, I hope Parker comes up with the real killer soon. But who could it be?"

This question got no reaction from the again-lethargic Farfel, so Joe tried another one. "What about one of the other partners?"

Farfel chuckled and then replied, "Hell, most of them stood to gain rather than lose if Halsey took over. He was a goose just about to drop a golden egg. And you could see them salivating in anticipation."

"Yes, I infer that's true of most of them," Joe agreed. "Of course, there are also those like Calvin Caldwell. He didn't seem to care about those possible profits."

"Caldwell?" Aaron shot back in a voice that cracked on the first syllable of the name. He hesitated and then asked, "Why Caldwell? I, I can't see any connection there. Why . . . that just makes no sense at all."

Joe could only stare at the frightened man, trying unsuccessfully to puzzle out what lay behind this outburst.

* * *

Anyone who had seen Karl after he left the tennis courts would have concluded the man was acting peculiarly. He was, first of all, muttering to himself and, in the process, keeping up a quite respectable one-man conversation. As he headed back to the hotel, Karl was saying, "Can't let Joe get too far out in front. I'll just stow my tennis gear at the room and then . . . yes, and then what?"

He nodded his head and answered his own question, "The scene of the crime, that's it. I'll check out the scene. That's the place to start."

He rounded a corner and, head down and still muttering, nearly bumped into two elderly ladies out for a stroll. The women shook their heads and agreed he was acting just like their equally elderly husbands often did.

Karl rounded another corner leading to one of the hotel's verandas and, spotting something that surprised him, he leapt back behind the corner. Sneaking a quick look, he confirmed what he thought he'd seen: it was Mrs. Bertram and Mary Margaret having drinks at an open-air bar on the veranda.

"Dare I say 'birds in the hand,'" Karl whispered to himself. "The scene of the crime must wait, for here are two real, live suspects."

103

Drawing himself up to his full height, he sauntered around the corner and acted as if he'd seen the two women for the first time. Approaching their table, Karl said, "Oh, good morning. What a pleasant surprise."

"Professor Teasdale," Mrs. Bertram responded.

"What good luck," Mary Margaret added. "Won't you join us and settle a problem in economics?"

"The good fortune must be mine," Karl replied as he quickly took a chair. And, not waiting to hear whatever question was troubling the two women, he asked, "I don't suppose you've heard any news about Halsey's murder? Have they caught the villain?"

"We've just been arguing a good case for why the real villain was Halsey himself."

Karl looked puzzled. "Halsey himself?" he asked.

"It was all his own fault," Mary Margaret complained. "Why'd he want to come over here and try to buy out our little magazine anyway? Why couldn't he just stay in Britain and buy something there?"

"Mary Margaret and I," Mrs. Bertram explained, "have been lamenting the irony of Lord Halsey's sudden interest in international business. It was just about as unfortunate for us as for him, what with the trials it's caused the partnership. We just can't see why he'd want to do it in the first place."

Karl waved his hand as if the problem were a minor one. "It's the strength of the dollar abroad and the resultant high rate of return on investments in America. Besides, the U.S. is a big market, as well. But let me tell you my theory about the murder."

"I never could understand this stuff about trading with other countries," Mary Margaret cut in. "Calvin is always preaching to me about how other countries are getting the better of us. You know, all those cheap Japanese cars and TVs and stereos sold in the U.S. And the cheap, subsidized foreign steel that's ruining our steel industry. Calvin gripes about that, too."

"Yes," Karl agreed. "I'm certain he would, but that's not what got Halsey killed. He—"

"Yet that's not the worst of it," Mary Margaret went on. "After I thought I understood it from Calvin, I read where U.S. Steel Corporation was buying some of that same foreign steel for their own construction projects. Now where's the logic in that?"

Karl was trapped. "They were simply acting like a rational consumer," he explained in resignation. "They were buying at the lowest possible price. Look at it this way: if the citizens of foreign countries are willing to tax themselves to subsidize their nation's steel exports, Americans would be foolish *not* to buy their favorably priced goods."

"Even if it means a loss of jobs in the American steel industry?"

"The Law of Comparative Advantage says each country should specialize in the production for export of those goods it can produce with the greatest relative advantage in comparison with other countries. *And* each country should import rather than produce at home those goods for which other countries have a comparative advantage. The end results of doing this are that, first, the volume of total world trade is maximized and, second, each individual country secures the maximum benefit from its trade relations. If America no longer has a comparative advantage in producing steel, there's always another good where we do."

"I wonder what an unemployed steelworker would say to that argument," Mrs. Bertram mused.

"No doubt there are short-term adjustment costs when a nation loses its former advantage in producing a given good. But the alternative is to pursue a hopeless situation of inefficiency and lack of competitiveness. We must face the economic facts in situations like that. As Peter Grace of the Grace Commission likes to say, that's the 'net net.'"

"That sounds dreadfully cold and harsh," Mary Margaret concluded.

"Yet the long-run economic benefits of accepting such

facts and following the Law of Comparative Advantage are enormous. And besides, our government has typically softened the economic blow of these changes. We—you and I as taxpayers—have supported uncompetitive industries like steel and auto manufacturing through millions of dollars of government subsidies of one kind or another. The political clout of those industries has meant that we have underwritten their inefficiencies."

"I infer you have no sympathy for those subsidies," Mrs. Bertram observed.

"Let me put it this way. If Lord Halsey had needed, and had gotten, a subsidy from the British government to make his effort to take over Arsgratia competitive, you would have thought that a foolish and unnecessary investment on the part of his government. You might have said something like: if he can't go it alone, why should the government subsidize him? Shouldn't we feel the same way, say, of the Detroit automakers? If the Japanese can make a better car and sell it for less, why should we try to limit their sales in America? Why not instead just put our displaced auto workers to building something where we have a comparative advantage?"

"Oh, I suppose you're correct," Mrs. Bertram agreed. "But, then, you are the economist." And, glancing at her watch, she added, "Goodness! Just look at the time. I'm overdue at the beauty salon. Come along, Mary Margaret, you can help me decide how to salvage the remainder of our shareholders' meeting. We've many wounded egos to patch, I fear."

"But, I—" Karl tried to say.

"Yes, Professor, I'm certain there's much more we really ought to know about international trade. But, perhaps another time."

They departed, leaving Karl muttering once again to himself.

Eleven

"I keep thinking about the concept of efficient markets," Karl was saying. "That is, where investors use all known, relevant, and available information to establish security values."

"How odd," Joe retorted. "I was thinking of the hotel's beef Wellington myself. I've seen the menu *du jour.*"

Appropriate at least to Joe's remark, the two men were strolling toward the Tiffany Dining Room for their evening meal. While Joe's anticipation of the food might have been higher, both were eager for the company they expected. Although Karl, for the moment, had something else on his mind.

"Yes," Karl continued, undeterred by his friend's reply, "people's behavior when they are *unaware* of all relevant information would differ, of course, from that when they are aware of it."

"Hmm, I suppose I have read that somewhere," Joe replied, pretending to search the deep recesses of his brain for some glimmer of the idea.

Karl fumed at this reply. "Don't be coy!" he shot back. "You know—" he started to say, but then he stopped in midsentence. Controlling his anger, Karl asked, presumably starting on a new tack, "If you don't want to talk about work, well then, how was your day?"

"Good, quite good."

"Did you sunbathe?" Karl asked.

"Oh, no. I wasn't in the mood for sun."

"Play any bridge?"

"No, I wasn't 'up' for bridge, as they say."

"Hmm." Karl was considering his next question. "So, eh," he began carefully, "how did you spend your day? I certainly got in a lot of tennis myself."

"Oh, I just puttered about."

Karl reddened a little in anger, but he decided to try once more. "Meet anybody in particular?" he asked.

"No, not in particular."

Now Karl was entirely hot. "Darn it, Joe! You're doing this on purpose."

"Doing what?" his friend asked with wide-eyed innocence. They had just arrived at the entrance to the dining room, so Joe added, as well, while they waited for the *maitre d'*, "Lovely room, don't you think? Those are Tiffany skylights in the ceiling." Joe pretended to study the large room and its elegant appointments, but the ruse was obvious and only made Karl madder.

"You're being evasive, that's what!" Karl almost shouted. "And you know perfectly well what you're doing. It's like I tried to say a minute ago about market efficiency." Here Karl stopped, uncertain of how he wanted to go on.

"Yes?" Joe prompted.

Evidently Karl hated to admit his position, but at last he said, "Well, it's this bet we have. Over the Apple stock. Now you set the bet and the stakes. And, as I recall explicitly, it had nothing to do with *who* figured out the murderer first. It was entirely about the motive."

"Yes, so?"

"So? So what did you learn today, of course? I've no doubt you spent the day sleuthing about, poking in keyholes, getting friendly with hotel maids and various suspects."

Joe stopped in mid-stride to react with exaggerated surprise, "*Moi?*"

"Yes, *vous*. And don't try any more of that on me, or I'll

give you back a different kind of French. Now I am right, am I not? You were sleuthing around today, weren't you?"

Joe rose to his full five-foot-five and said in mock indignation, "I object to the word 'sleuthing.' I was merely being a scientist."

"Oh, yes, I see, just gathering data to test your theory, is that it?"

"But of course."

"So we're back to where *I* started," Karl said with satisfaction. "Back to information, that is. For we both need adequate data—or information—to test our theories just like an efficient investor needs it to make the optimal decision."

"Do I surmise, Professor Teasdale," his friend began, "that—dare I use that awful phrase—the 'bottom line' of your inquisitiveness is simply 'what did I learn today relevant to the murder?'"

"At last! The light dawns," Karl lamented.

"In truth, plain and simple, then, not much. But—" here Joe had to raise his hand to stifle Karl's newly aroused anger at this seeming verbal evasion. Then Joe quickly added, "But I will tell every bit of that 'not much.' Although, since here we are at the restaurant and our host and hostess are waiting, I suppose it had better be over after-dinner drinks."

Karl frowned but accepted this logic. "Oh, all right. But in the meantime I trust you appreciate my cleverness in securing us this dinner invitation with the Caldwells. We ought to be able to learn something useful tonight, too."

Joe nodded in agreement and, as the *maitre d'* led them across the dining room to the Caldwells' table, he asked of Karl in an aside, "Indeed, I am impressed by your getting us this invitation. However did you manage it?"

With some surprise Karl replied, "Why I saw Mary Margaret at the tennis courts. So I simply up and asked her."

"How exceedingly clever!" his companion whispered back, but the reply was lost in the noise of their arrival at the table.

* * *

Calvin Caldwell was in a particularly jovial mood. When Joe and Karl arrived at the table, Calvin and Mary Margaret were laughing. And, as both professors observed, the couple was just about to finish a bottle of champagne. But Caldwell rose to greet them and, at the same time, signal the waiter to bring another bottle.

After the initial "good evenings" and "how are you's" had gone around the table, there followed a brief and awkward moment of silence. Mary Margaret, Karl, and Joe looked at each other, knowing what subject was uppermost in all their minds, but each one seemingly afraid to broach it. Then Calvin glanced up from studying the menu, saw their expressions, and chuckled. Raising his glass, he said eagerly, "A toast." And, as the others reached for their glasses, he added, "Here's to crime!" Then he laughed heartily.

From behind his inscrutable, owl-eyed countenance Joe Birnoff decided Caldwell was perhaps more intelligent than he'd first thought. The man had certainly intuited what the other three of them had been thinking. Now if only—but Joe's drift into private thought was interrupted by Calvin's next line.

". . . that you two are probably just like my wife," Caldwell was saying as Joe became fully conscious again. "I actually had to scare up a golf game today to get away from her constant talking about who might have done old Halsey in."

Mary Margaret reddened and tried to defend herself, but Calvin stopped her with a touch on the arm so he could go on. "Not yet, you'll get your chance," he admonished. Then he added, "You two professors are about the only ones at the hotel she hasn't suspected yet. But given enough time, you might even get on her list."

"It's natural curiosity," his wife finally got in. "After all, I've never been so close to a . . . a, well, such a thing before. It's just like in the movies."

110

"My colleague here," Karl offered dryly to Calvin, "has, I fear, been stricken with the same malady. He is, however, by his nature a quiet man." Here Karl paused to give Joe a reproachful look before adding, "Thus, he keeps his speculations to himself."

"Lucky you!" Calvin replied.

"Where's the fun in not talking about it?" Mary Margaret joked.

"Indeed," Karl said. And then to Joe he added, "Have you no sense of fun?"

"Yeah," Mary Margaret agreed. "Where's your—" she began, and then she hiccuped, as much to her own as everyone else's surprise. "Oops. It's the champagne, I guess," she added with embarrassment.

Joe was taking this ribbing well, smiling at each new remark. But he also saw an opening to turn the conversation in a different direction, for he now said, "I certainly admit I find the murder interesting. That's only natural. I'll bet even your curiosity has been raised a bit by it, Calvin. Don't you have any guesses about 'who dun it'?"

"Probably the butler," Calvin replied with a laugh.

"Oh, no imagination," Mary Margaret scolded, sounding just a little drunk.

"Yes, that's no serious guess," Joe agreed.

"All right, then," Caldwell admitted, and with a smile he offered, "Maybe it was our boy Aaron. After all, he had the best motive. Halsey would've fired him if he got control of the company, and they'd already had that fight."

"In which Mr. Farfel was soundly beaten, I recall," Joe rebutted. "He hardly appeared capable, based on that particular round of fisticuffs, of tossing the late Lord Halsey off his balcony."

Calvin laughed again. "Maybe he *scared* Halsey off the balcony. You know, threatened to kiss him—or worse—if he didn't jump himself."

"Calvin!" his wife exclaimed, but he ignored her to go on.

111

"Who knows? Halsey was a tough businessman. You make enemies when you're like that. It could have been anybody."

"It could even have been you then. Or maybe Mary Margaret," Joe said meekly.

That remark rocked Caldwell. His head went back and his anger showed in his eyes. But he caught himself and mastered the reaction. Then he leaned forward, smiled, and said, "Yeah, but she didn't."

That exchange broke the playful mood of the conversation. And it left them all at least momentarily uncomfortable. Joe broke eye contact with Calvin by taking another sip of champagne. Mary Margaret fingered the stem of her glass. Even Calvin looked away, pretending to survey the room and its other occupants.

It was Karl, however, who saw a way out of this difficult predicament. He fished the second champagne bottle from its ice bucket to study the label. And then he asked, "Tell me something about how the so-called other half lives. Is it the case that rich Texas oilmen drink imported champagne every night? Or, as would be the case with most of the rest of us, are we celebrating some important occasion?"

Calvin responded with a very odd smile. It was a smile that was part proud adolescent and part roguish adult. Calvin even relished the pleasure of that smile for what seemed like a good half-minute before finally saying, "Oh, just a neat little business deal. Nothing all that big, right, Mary Margaret? But clever, nonetheless. I always say that's what makes a successful businessman. He seizes on every opportunity—big or little—and makes them all pay off for what they're worth."

"Another gusher of oil from some otherwise unrewarding stretch of Texas desert?" Karl asked with obviously fading interest. No doubt, he expected to hear more about just how smart practical businessmen were—without the help of economists.

Calvin smiled his complex smile again, and then he said, "Admittedly that would have been more profitable, but no, it was nothing like that. Yet I did spend this afternoon buying out most of the other Arsgratia partners."

Joe choked on his last swallow of champagne. Even the usually unflappable Karl raised his eyebrows and responded, "My word! Now that's quite a turn."

"Yeah, who'd have guessed it, right?" Calvin agreed.

"But . . . ," Karl obviously started to ask why, but he caught himself in mid-thought. Then he nodded and said, "Of course. You want their tax losses."

Calvin chuckled. "You boys hang around long enough and you'll learn even more good business sense."

"So you'll maintain the present philosophy of the magazine," Joe put in, "along with its inevitable financial losses."

Calvin looked at his wife and then back to the professor. He spread his hands wide and said, "Art for art's sake, Doc. And, the way I got it figured, I plan for the magazine to lose three or four times as much next year. If you're gonna take tax losses, you might as well take big ones." Then, with his odd smile, Calvin concluded, "Ain't capitalism grand, Doc!"

Joe could only shake his head.

"Hell, Doc," Calvin said in defense, "I didn't write the tax laws."

"Oh, for the flat tax plan!" Karl lamented. And then, more charitably, he added, "No, you didn't write the laws. But little economic good comes of many of their features—like those that allow such inflated write-offs."

"They certainly save me a lot of money—like with this very one," Calvin replied.

"True enough, but it's both inequitable and inefficient," Karl argued.

"Inequitable!" was Mary Margaret's slightly inebriated response. "That means unfair. What's unfair if Calvin saves on his taxes?"

Karl didn't know whether he should take her question seriously or not, but after a moment's hesitation he responded like a true academic. "This, like many other unfortunate features of the present system—call them loopholes or tax subsidies or whatever you will—destroys what we economists call 'horizontal equity.' Such equity would exist if people making the same total income paid the same amount in taxes. That would seem fair, now wouldn't it?"

"But just one little old write-off for Arsgratia," Mary Margaret wheedled.

"Yes, and a tax shelter here, a tax-exempt security there, special treatment of capital gains another place, and . . . well, I'll not go on, but the list is a rather long one. As a result, we have very little horizontal equity. Why . . . why many people take such advantage of those provisions that they pay no income tax at all."

"That's not fair!" their hostess said quite loudly, and Karl had to wonder whether she was shifting her argumentative ground or just losing control to the alcohol. "Yes," he agreed. "I believe that's where I came in on this subject."

"Maybe it's not fair," Calvin agreed. "But it sure is good business. Like I said, look at what your so-called loopholes save me and my companies in taxes."

Karl really bristled at this idea. "On the contrary, I could hardly disagree more vigorously. It's quite bad business instead."

"Oh, yeah?" Calvin shot back angrily. "I suppose this so-called flat tax we've heard so much about and that you mentioned earlier *and* that would probably cost me higher taxes is better, huh?"

Karl responded with a bit of heat himself. "Whether it would cost you more in taxes is dependent on how the rates would be structured *and* on how many junk investments you now have," Karl pointed out.

"Junk investments?" Calvin and Mary Margaret asked together.

"Yes, those whose primary value is the tax saving they generate rather than their productive return. Almost all the various tax shelters that high-bracket taxpayers invest in would qualify. Things like buying up Arabian horses or certain real estate investments. Or, for that matter, Arsgratia shares."

"But that's art, not junk!" Mary Margaret protested.

"I may not know art," Joe Birnoff put in, "but with some of this modern stuff, I sometimes wonder just whether it is art or junk."

"Our different aesthetic tastes aside," Karl went on, "I wager you would not have bought those shares, Calvin, if they had no tax loss value."

"Of course not. I'm no fool."

"Except as the tax system makes fools of many of us," Karl lamented. "If it were not for that inducement, your money would have been invested in other projects with the potential for benefiting not only yourself but the economy at large."

"But how's the flat tax gonna fix that?" Mary Margaret asked, now beginning noticeably to slur her words.

Karl sighed and took a deep breath. He seemed to be considering the wisdom of going on when half his audience was in a questionable state for following the argument. But he evidently thought the question too important to be left unanswered, even for this audience. "It would do so if the bulk of the loopholes were eliminated," he said. "Just as most proponents of the plan have argued they should be. And bringing down the high tax rates in the progressive scale for individuals would help. Then there'd be less inducement to seek shelters in the first place."

"I could go for bringing down the rates," Calvin admitted.

"See, there are some attractive features to the proposal. Another one is that we wouldn't need all those CPAs and tax accountants anymore."

"Now you've really got my interest, son," Calvin responded. "You can't imagine how I dislike accountants."

"Somehow, I suspect he can," Joe interjected, and the

look Karl shared with his colleague indicated Birnoff was right.

"Under the simplest form of a flat tax—and with the rate that many people believe would bring in at least as much revenue as the present system," Karl continued, "you'd simply add up all your income for the year, multiply the total by twenty percent, and then pay the resulting amount as your tax."

"Hell, even Mary Margaret could handle that!" Calvin almost shouted.

"Imagine!" Joe mused. "It'd even be a nonsexist tax system."

Calvin looked puzzled, but then he failed to get the joke—of which he was the butt.

"I trust you see now," Karl concluded, "why I say the present tax system is inequitable and why it distorts the investment decisions of both individuals and corporations. In one sense relative to this issue Lord Halsey actually did me and my argument a service. His proposal to turn *Artworld* into a profitable venture points up very clearly the contrast between businesses run for profit and those run for their losses. Or, for that matter, the contrast with those that simply are ill-run and are, therefore, not very profitable. Our present tax system encourages far too much of the latter two kinds of business at the expense of the first and, hence, at the expense of economic efficiency and productivity, as well."

"I would argue, on the other hand," Joe Birnoff now interjected, "that Lord Halsey did Calvin here an even bigger favor."

Calvin smiled slyly at Joe and then asked, "And just how do you figure that, Doc?"

"Oh, it's quite simple. Before Halsey came along I wager the partners were content to lose money every year as patrons of art. But when he showed them there was an alternative that promised high profits where at least some of their commitment to art might be maintained, many of them became disenchanted. Yet Mrs. Bertram and a few of her

116

trusted supporters—like the two of you, I surmise—hold enough shares to keep the magazine on its old course now that Halsey's threat is eliminated. And, to make it even more favorable for you—"

"So he set the situation up for me," Calvin interrupted. "They're unhappy knowing both that they could be making a profit *and* that they will not be doing so. So I buy them out, buying up their tax losses for myself. *And* if I increase the losses the magazine incurs, I even get a bigger tax loss."

"Such as?" Karl requested.

"First, I'll spend about fifty thousand dollars getting those shares. Imagine! Fifty grand for shares of an outfit that can't turn a profitable dime. Then, I figure that after I get Farfel to running the magazine the way I want, that is, when it's losing even more money, then I'll get at least a three-to-one tax write-off in return. For my fifty grand investment, that's a hundred and fifty grand paper loss for me as a partner, *and*, because I'm in a fifty-percent tax bracket, a seventy-five grand tax savings that I purchased for only fifty. Not bad, huh?"

"Indeed," was all Karl could respond.

"And it keeps my wife happy to boot," Caldwell added.

"As I said," Joe put in, "Lord Halsey certainly did you a favor. First, as you put it, by 'setting the situation up' for you. And second, by being so conveniently murdered."

In response to that comment Calvin Caldwell's proud smile turned to something far less cheerful.

Twelve

"Out with it, dammit!" Detective Parker was shouting. "This time I want the truth. It's not Teasdale and Birnoff, now is it? You two are really a modern-day Holmes and Watson, now aren't you?"

Joe and Karl winced. They sat, almost cowering, in the bare, hard chairs in the hole of an office Parker kept at the hotel. Parker, on the other hand, was lumbering about the room, shouting angrily, and pausing only to lean over one or the other of the two men from time to time and shake his finger at them. It was, as Joe Birnoff managed to think despite his embarrassment, an impressive performance. Here was one big man who really knew how to use his size to good effect.

"The trouble is," Parker was saying, "I can't decide which of you's supposed to be the clever Holmes and which the bumbling Watson. I think I've got two Watsons on my hands."

"But Detect—" Joe attempted to say.

"Quiet! I'm not finished. I'm mad, and you two are gonna suffer it awhile, because you two could have messed up everything. What with your stumbling around the hotel like a pair of bloodhounds in heat, putting everybody and his third cousin on their guard."

Parker stopped to catch his breath, and then he said with renewed vigor, "You, Teasdale. You and your grilling of the

118

hotel maids. You almost cost me some of my best witnesses. *And* the hotel half its staff. Hell, they're probably illegals anyway. The last person they want to talk to is a cop—or anybody who acts like one. And your little idea of trying to trace Halsey's movements that last day. That went over real well, too. There you had the restaurant crew, the maids, *and* half the recreational staff with their backs up. I've got three of my men out there now trying to undo your damage so maybe those witnesses will talk to *us* again."

Parker turned away and walked across the room. He swung his leg backwards as if he were about to kick a chair in front of him. Then he grunted like a weight lifter and swung the leg forward. The two professors steeled themselves for the crash, but Parker stopped the swinging foot just before it met its target. Instead of kicking the chair, he simply whispered, "Damn."

The detective stared fixedly at the chair he'd wanted to destroy, trying to control his temper. That break in the man's tirade was just long enough for Joe to glance over at Karl, smile, and whisper, "Been getting in a lot of tennis, eh?"

Joe thought Teasdale's dressing down had actually been a touch funny. After all, how often did he get to see his friend's haughty superiority punctured? But Joe had to smile, as well, over how clever, if still bumbling as Parker had put it, his colleague had been. Why hadn't he thought of retracing Halsey's steps on that last day?

Joe's amusement was short-lived, however, for Parker heard the whispered remark and caught the professor's smile out of the corner of his eye. "Ha!" the detective cried, renewing his attack. "So you think it's funny, do you, Professor Birnoff? Like to see your buddy squirm, huh? Well, you'd better nail your can to your own chair."

Parker advanced on Joe, probably knowing the impact his looming bulk could have on so short a man. He looked down on Joe, exhaled slowly—his nostrils flaring—and then said, "And weren't you the cute one yourself? Playing the seemingly confused and well-intentioned buddy with some of the key

119

suspects. Trying to lull them into one of those 'false senses of security,' I guess, in hopes that they'd say something incriminating. Was that supposed to be your Lieutenant Columbo routine? Well, it may play in Hollywood, but it doesn't here."

After this attack on Joe, Parker appeared to have exhausted his energy if not his anger. He blew out a big breath, and then he crossed the room to slouch into the chair behind his desk.

"Jeez," he muttered. Then he added, "And don't go feeling sorry for yourselves. This little chat is nothing like the one we'd of had if you two *had* blown my case."

"Your, eh, case?" Karl asked warily.

Parker caught the inference and shot back, "Yeah, my case. My case which is now closed, so to speak. You see, I've arrested the murderer. Or murderers, as it just may prove."

The two professors were stunned. Karl pulled himself up erectly and arched his eyebrows as if he were thinking: Oh, so now you tell us. And Joe fired off another round of rapid-fire blinking while he began to pat his pockets.

From his erect, wounded-dignity pose Karl asked, "And who, might I be so bold to inquire, have you determined to have been the perpetrator?"

Parker looked up at them and broke into a wide grin. "Oh, yeah. Watson and Watson are just dying to know how we did it, aren't you? Well listen real close, take good notes, and let's see if you can get this straight the first time through. At the end, there just might be a pop quiz."

Karl bristled at the man's words, but Parker didn't see the reaction. The detective had looked down at his desk, composing his thoughts and deciding where to begin. Then he looked up and said bluntly, "It was that kid the tennis assistant. Chuck Stone's his name. Him and that Helga woman, the wife. Although we're not clear yet whether she was an active participant or just an accessory. But after a day or two of chatting right nice with them both, then we'll know. You can put money on that."

"The tennis assistant!" Karl repeated in considerable surprise.

"Yes, the tennis assistant," Parker said again with emphasis, as if to a slow-learning pupil.

"The way we figure it," Parker went on, "Halsey had found out about this little affair between those two. Maybe he was suspicious of his wife from the beginning. But, then, who wouldn't have been? Anyway, the evidence suggests he tried to catch them in the act, so to speak, and there was a fight in the apartment. It's also clear young Chuck was blackmailing Helga, probably threatening to reveal her infidelities to her husband. Maybe Halsey had figured that out, too. But as I was saying, Halsey caught the two of them in the apartment, there was a fight, and one or both of them threw him over the balcony."

Karl arched his eyes at this explanation, and Parker saw the gesture. "You don't see it, Professor? Want to hear my evidence? And why not? It'll be a lesson in real detective work. You see, it really wasn't hard. Nothing sensational, no Holmes and Watson stuff. It was just everyday *professional* detecting.

"The scene of the crime, you see, gave us a lot of information. There'd been a hell of a fight in the apartment. The furniture was all tossed around and broken up. But there were signs that something entirely different had been going on, too. Like a mattress pulled out on the balcony. And those towels that had covered the balcony railings, making it into something of an intimate little spot.

"Oh, and did I tell you about the fingerprints? Well, there were Halsey's, and Helga's, and Chuckie boy's, and that woman Bertram's. We knew she had been there that morning, too. But, then, she admitted that. And there were a couple of other interesting things. There was an athlete's sweatband in Halsey's pocket. And on the floor of the apartment, buried in the mess, there was an envelope with five thousand dollars in cash in it."

Parker stopped to make eye contact with one and then the other of the two professors, and he asked, "Now, I'm not going

121

too fast for you fellows, am I?" He paused an instant, giving the appearance of waiting for a reply, but actually just to enjoy his own sarcasm. Then he continued.

"So that's where we began. And naturally we checked out all the possible angles. And some of those angles led to some fascinating stuff. Like that five k. It wasn't hard to find where so much money had come from. Helga had cashed that amount of traveler's checks the day before. And she'd gotten another five grand just a few days earlier, but that's getting ahead of my story. Well, we didn't know it at the time, but when the lab report came back, dear sweet Helga had the only fingerprints—besides those of the hotel cashier—that had made it onto all those bills.

"So we checked Helga a little further, and buried in her lingerie drawer—and what lingerie, fellows. But buried in that drawer was a phone message the hotel operator had transcribed for her. It read: 'H. See you at noon on Thursday. And bring ten k this time. C.'"

Parker studied the two professors again and then asked, "Cute, huh? So naturally we began to check out young Chuckie boy. And you know what we found next? Hidden away in his gym locker was another note. And this one read: 'Come to the usual place at twelve for special *liebe*. Be not late.' I guess I don't have to tell two smart guys like you that *liebe* is German for love. Oh, and there's more. Down in the bottom of that same locker, in a pile of dirty tennis clothes, was another envelope with five thousand dollars in it. And you know what? Oh, I bet you clever guys already guessed. Helga's prints were the only ones on that money, too."

Parker leaned back in his chair and smiled a broad, tooth-baring smile. Then he said, "I presume you two can put it all together from there, right?"

Karl could manage only an offended, or perhaps hurt, look in response to the question. He turned to his friend, who seemed to be just coming out of one of his mental trances. Joe shrugged at Karl and then said, "The tennis assistant and the wife. Somehow I never . . ."

But Karl had just thought of a question, so he turned back to Parker to ask, "Why is it that you're undecided about the role Halsey's wife played?"

"Simple logic based on the facts at the scene," the officer said flatly. "It would have been quite difficult for a woman, even a strong one, to win a struggle like must have been going on and then push a man over that balcony."

"I see," Karl replied. "Just to have the power to rip loose the railing in the process, that would seem unusual even in a man."

"Don't make too much of that. Those balconies are actually kind of weak. They're designed to tear away in high winds—like in a hurricane—so that the main structure of the building won't be damaged by their wrenching action. We've actually had people rip them off by accident, by silly horseplay or by just pushing hard on them when they thought the railings were stronger than they are. But as I was saying, it would still require a man's strength—both to rip out the railing and to throw someone over. Of course, Helga just may have been giving Chuckie an extra hand, so to speak, in the process."

"That means, those last remarks of yours mean, that is," Joe interrupted, "that they haven't confessed. Am I correct?"

Parker shrugged and replied, "That's true, not that it's important. But how did you—"

Now it was Joe's turn to interrupt. "If they had confessed, you wouldn't have to be making inferences based on the physical possibilities at the scene of the crime. Simple logic, you might say."

Parker missed the dig, but Karl didn't leave him much time to consider it. The professor asked, "Just what are their stories? Helga and Chuck, that is."

Parker waved his hand as if swatting away a pesky fly. "Aw, it's the typical stuff you expect at first. They're both amazed that we could suspect them. They think it's incredible. They know nothing about it. And then, after a little thought, they come back with: 'I was nowhere near the apartment. You're trying to frame me. I don't even have to talk to you. I got my rights.'"

Parker shook his head, chuckled, and went on, "So we tell them some of our evidence, talking to them separately this whole time, you see. But we tell them just a little, sort of to tease 'em and see what they say. And then we get: 'Well, so what if I *was* there that morning. But I really wasn't there. The door was locked and I couldn't get in.' Next we hear: 'You found *what* in my locker? You guys *are* trying to frame me! I've seen this on TV.'"

"They're being—" Joe and Karl said simultaneously, and then, in surprise at apparently having the same thought, they stopped and looked at each other with amusement.

"Let me ask him," Karl said. And, turning back to Parker, he asked, "You say they've been interrogated separately?"

"Yes."

"For very long?"

Parker hesitated, not sure what to make of this question, but then he answered, "I guess they both spent about six hours in interrogation."

"Six hours!" Karl was flabbergasted. "Isn't that unusually long?"

Parker only shrugged in response.

"And did you try all the usual tricks on them?" Joe put in.

"Tricks?" Parker was suspicious.

"Yes, like on TV?"

"Oh, yeah," the officer replied wearily. "We used all the tricks, just like on TV."

"Including offering each one leniency, like a reduced charge, if he—or she—would confess and inform on the other?"

"What'd I just say?" Parker came back with some heat. "I said it was just like on the damned television."

Joe and Karl shared one of their pregnant-with-secret-meaning looks. And Joe concluded, "So they deny everything and neither will confess."

"Yeah. Both of them say they weren't in the apartment. They know nothing of the money. They didn't kill him."

Another mental light bulb went on in Joe's head in response to this remark and he quickly said, "It must be difficult for Helga to deny knowing about the money. After all, you said hers were the only fingerprints on it."

Parker shrugged again. "I tell you this is typical. They just don't know how much we've got on them, so they're trying to bluff their way along. With the money, she claims she cashed those traveler's checks for her husband when he was too busy. Then she'd give him the money. That's real good, huh? 'Cause he's not here to deny it. On account of him being dead, he can't counter that argument. But don't you Doctor Watsons worry. The more the typical suspect tries to bluff his way along, the more mistakes he makes. Especially when he doesn't know all the stuff that *we* know. They trap themselves after a while."

Joe was satisfied to jot down a note and stare fixedly at it after this last comment. But Karl had another question, and after a glance at his friend he asked Parker, "I suppose . . . I suppose your reconstruction of the crime means that, if you are correct, this was a crime of passion. Caught in *flagrante delicto* by the husband, a nasty scene escalated into a fight and . . . and so on. Thus it was not likely, I surmise, based on this scenario, that this was a premeditated, or . . . or rational crime in any sense."

Parker looked hard at Karl, trying to decipher the motive behind this question. But the professor offered no clue, so Parker only answered, "I suppose that's fair. Although I hardly think of crime—particularly murder—as ever rational. You know we burn people in this state for murder."

"Burn them?" Karl responded.

"Yeah. You know, the electric chair."

"Oh, yes, that. But you see we economists have a conception of rationality that distinguishes the wisdom of a given decision from the manner in which it was reached. If it followed a certain mental process, it was rational. Even if it proves unwise after the fact. And we apply that concept of rationality to some criminal behavior. I was just trying to decide whether it might fit this particular criminal act."

Karl glanced again at Joe. And Joe was now listening quite intently to the conversation.

"Any rational person, if you asked me," Parker was saying dogmatically, "would never commit murder. Not in this state."

"Ah, but perhaps that's because you perceive the odds of getting caught as higher than many murderers do," Karl explained. "Again, that's in part a matter of the wisdom of the decision and not the manner in which it was made. Because we live in a world of uncertainty and less than perfect knowledge, many of our rationally arrived at decisions may still turn out to have been unwise ones. We were, in those instances, simply wrong about the facts—or the odds—that we included in the calculation of our decision. In this instance you just might know the odds better than do many would-be murderers. After all, it is your business. You are an insider, so to speak." Turning to Joe, Karl added to his friend, "It's like the semistrong form of market efficiency, wouldn't you agree?" And then, to the detective again, he said, "Your attitude about crime may also arise in part because you are *crime averse.*"

"I'm what?"

"Crime averse. That means that as you go about seeking to maximize your utility or your satisfaction," here Karl saw the puzzled look on Parker's face and added, "in other words, as you seek to achieve various goals in your life, you will resort to illegal means only when the benefits are extraordinarily high. High enough, that is, to overcome a strong disposition *not* to commit a crime. That's what crime averse means. Now a *crime-neutral* person would weigh each possible means to his desired end equally. That is, simple legality or illegality would not in and of themselves matter to such a person. Only the perceived costs and benefits of each means would be important."

Karl stopped to see how Parker was responding to these ideas, and then he went on, "And there's a third type, the *crime preferrer*. Such a person would eliminate the legal alternatives in favor of the illegal ones, where you would do the opposite. Surely in your business you've met many people like that."

"I suppose so, but I still don't see how all this is getting us to rational crime."

Now it was Karl's turn to frown at the slow-witted pupil. "If you accept the existence of those different types of people," he said, "the rest should be obvious. The likelihood of criminal behavior by a crime-neutral person, for example, is determined just like the behavior of the rational consumer."

"You mean they decide whether to buy a little crime or not?" Parker joked.

"I mean that, just as the rational consumer attempts to maximize his satisfaction by getting the most product for the lowest possible cost, the rational crime-neutral person will choose an illegal route to his goal when its perceived satisfaction-to-cost ratio exceeds that of all the other possible ones, legal or illegal. The same situation even holds for a crime-averse person except that the perceived satisfaction or benefit of a criminal act would have to be very much higher to induce him—or her—to choose it over a legal one. And in both cases there is the qualification, recall, that the satisfactions and costs may not always be perceived correctly. Although there is evidence they are so perceived at least a good deal of the time."

Parker leaned back in his chair and cast a wary look at Karl. Then he asked, "You think all that gobbledegook really means anything? Even if somebody just might do all that calculating, I can't see that it happens very much. How do you know people really think that way?"

Karl rose up to his full height, taking offense as Parker would soon learn at this slight against his profession. "Economic research on crime," Karl began, "has found considerable evidence to support this position. That research has shown crime rates to be inversely related to the risk of arrest and punishment, as well as to the severity of the punishment. In other words, crime rates are lower where the joint risk, or probability, of arrest and punishment is higher. Thus, you see, I'm certain, that crime rates are sensitive to risk and return. The perceived costs and benefits, furthermore, are sensitive to the actual costs and benefits. In consequence, because we can explain crime rates at least in part based on assumptions of rational behavior—taking account of economic motivations concerning risk and return—I believe it fair to conclude that criminal behavior is itself at least in part rationally motivated."

"All right, all right, I surrender," Parker almost pleaded. "So maybe it does work 'in part,' as you say. So what's it got to do with the present case?"

"What it's got to do with," Joe Birnoff put in with a laugh, "is ten shares of Apple Computer stock."

Thirteen

"For a few moments I thought Parker had us there," Joe was saying.

"Yes, by the, uh, neck, I guess one could say," Karl agreed. "Although my students have another anatomical term for it, I understand."

Joe Birnoff blinked in wonder. Barnyard biology was evidently not one of his intellectual strengths.

"Of course, if you hadn't been playing the sleuth so ineptly," Karl began.

"Me!" Joe rose up, practically to his toe-tips, in reaction. "What about *your* sneaking around, grilling the help, and—"

Karl tried to wave off this rebuttal, and he interrupted to say, "Parker exaggerated that. I was actually quite subtle, if I must say so myself."

"Well, somebody must have thought otherwise," Joe replied. Then Birnoff shook his head, laughed, and quoted once more, "'I've been getting in a lot of tennis myself.'"

"Oh, don't be a smart-ass!"

Joe laughed to himself and, also to himself, mumbled, "Ah, but I'm not the dumb-ass who brought it up." Recognizing the limits of his friend's tolerance, however, he let the subject drop.

The two men walked on in silence. They were strolling the bluffs along Clearwater Bay, "cooling down," as Karl had put it, from Detective Parker's tirade. As they walked Karl struck an obvious pose of being deep in thought—with his head down and his hands clasped behind his neck. Joe, too, was deep in thought or, rather, off in his own mental "third dimension." But Joe was still sending out periodic body signals—like an occasional nodding of his head at sights along their path or a seemingly involuntary shrugging of his shoulders as if he still were in touch with his strictly corporeal self and needs—all to hide the fact of his mind's absence from the immediate world around him.

"I must admit," Karl said after a few minutes of thought, "that my interest is more piqued than ever about the identity of the murderer."

Joe presumably had to float back through several galaxies of mental space to rejoin the conversation, for they walked on a few paces before he asked, "What's that about the murderer?"

"My interest. It's been piqued again by our little session with Detective Parker."

"Still worried about your theory holding up?" Joe asked with a twinkle in his eye and a sidelong glance at his friend.

"Hardly, as I suspect you already know. The man can't see the counterevidence that certainly throws *his* explanation into serious doubt."

"Indeed."

"It sounded like a textbook Prisoner's Dilemma if ever I heard one," Karl went on. "The fact that neither Chuck nor Helga pleaded guilty to a reduced charge leads me to believe that they aren't guilty. If they were, it would have been rational for both of them to plead guilty. Both should have feared the other one would confess first and leave them facing the stiffer sentence. After all, as the good detective said, Florida 'burns' people for murder."

"Yes," Joe agreed. "I believe this state has one of the nation's largest 'death row' populations. But Parker, he probably doesn't see the logic of the Prisoner's Dilemma because he's so hardened by the everyday experiences of being in law enforcement. You heard his assessment of what the typical

130

criminal is like. Just imagine what it'd be like if *you* had to spend all your life working with criminals."

"As opposed to students?" Karl's question sounded like the prospect might not be such an awful one in his judgment. But he wanted to pursue another thought, so he quickly added, "No, I don't believe that's the problem. At least not exactly. I think he suffers the same difficulty that Calvin Caldwell does."

Joe was intrigued. "How's that?"

"It's the narrow-mindedness and myopia of the supposedly practical man of business . . . or of policing or of what-have-you. They fall into narrow and short-sighted mental routines. Routines born of lazy habit and sanctified by the past successes or immediate results they've produced. Such people's minds close to innovation and to long-range goals—whether in ideas or in practice. And, worst of all, they forget that the very routines they do practice have their own basis in ideas. Ideas that were at one time current in their profession. Thus, they become fixed in their work habits, oblivious to the intellectual basis that justified those habits in the first place, rigidified against any possible change with the times, and inured against even the principle that ideas matter. And, in the quintessential American way, they exalt all this as the wondrous result of practicality. Practicality, the goddess of American professionalism."

Joe blinked at his friend and said, "That may be a bit harsh, but it's certainly marvelously stated. I trust I may use it, at least in a lecture."

"With the proper credit, of course."

"Of course."

They walked on in silence, both musing over Karl's indictment of the American mind. But it was not long before Joe went back to another thread in his friend's little speech.

"I infer you believe Parker to be hopeless, then."

"At least for the present," Karl agreed. "If he can't see the meaning of the Prisoner's Dilemma, then he's probably not sensitive to any evidence counter to his principal suspicions."

131

"I suppose we might continue our private efforts," Joe suggested, cocking an eye at his friend and adding as a qualification, "Very cautiously and circumspectly."

"And very *coordinatedly*," Karl shot back with emphasis. "I've no desire to sit through another of the man's harangues because of your bumbling about."

Joe let this remark pass, for his mind had jumped ahead to another point. "Suffering through that dressing-down did have its rewards, though," he said.

Karl's reaction—a fierce grimace—forced Joe to explain, "We learned what Parker knew that we didn't before. We heard his evidence."

"I can imagine a variety of more pleasant ways to have done so," Karl sniffed. Then, in a partial concession, he added, "Although I suppose it was useful. And there appear to be some obvious leads based on what he said. I believe my original hypothesis about motive still appears quite reasonable in light of some of the evidence from the apartment."

"Perhaps," was all Joe would concede.

"And if it was a matter of strength," Karl mused.

"Yes, that presumably narrows our list."

"Perhaps we should divide them between us and see what we can learn about each," Karl suggested.

"Just as long as it's entirely coordinated," Joe replied, again hoping to tweak his friend.

But Karl only said, "Entirely," and walked on.

This exchange seemingly amounted to a settled agreement, for neither man seemed to think it necessary to say more on the subject. But after a couple of minutes of silent strolling, Karl decided he had to raise one loose thread.

"There is one other interesting angle indicated by what we learned from Parker," he began.

Joe looked up at his friend, uncertain about just what this angle might be.

"It's Helga. If Parker's right, just for the sake of argument, then her role was pivotal. She's linked to the crime in several key ways. But . . . ," Karl paused, reviewing the detective's recital of the facts, and then concluded, "I'd like to hear Helga's side of the story."

Joe clasped his hands behind his back, made a funny little skip in his walk, and then asked, "Well, are you up for another game of tennis?"

Karl turned red and glowered at his friend.

* * *

Joe Birnoff was shaking his head as he got off the elevator and started down the hotel corridor. He still wasn't quite sure how—or why—Karl had talked him into this. True, he himself had been the one who first heard the rumor, which had been floating from table to table at lunch, that Helga was back at the hotel. Confined to her room under police supervision, that's what he'd finally put together from several different versions of the rumor. Something about respecting the rights of a foreign national until a grand jury had actually indicted her.

But Karl appeared the natural candidate for this interview, Joe thought. After all, Karl had been the one who'd played tennis with her. He was the one Helga had obviously taken an interest in. There was a natural *entrée* for Karl.

But Karl had resisted. He'd made up all manner of excuses. He'd said Joe was better at "that sort of thing," whatever "that sort of thing" was. He'd said ... But here was Helga's door, so Joe had to let those thoughts drop to greet the uniformed sheriff's officer lounging before it.

"Uh, Officer. Sir. I, uh," Joe was stammering for he was suddenly embarrassed. The pass. Where was the pass? He searched his pockets fruitlessly, while the sleepy eyed officer leaned against the door frame, chewing on a toothpick.

Joe looked up at the man and, while continuing to search his pockets, explained, "I have a pass from Detective Parker's office. Somewhere. It, uh, says I can see Mrs. Halsey."

The officer chewed on without a word.

133

"I had it just a moment ago."

In the finest tradition of classic lawman gestures, the officer reached up and grasped his toothpick while watching Joe with studied indifference. He directed the instrument toward some offending dental crevice, and then he removed it from his mouth to ask, "You Birnoff?" The name came out like "beer-nuff."

Joe blinked and, still searching his pockets, nodded and agreed, "The same."

"She's waitin'," was the officer's reply as he lazily opened the door with one hand—without moving from his slouch against its frame. "Parker says you can have upta a half hour. You ain't got a gun, have you?"

Joe looked startled, but the officer's practiced eye quickly executed the only "pat-down" that was necessary. "Nah, I didn't think so," the man concluded. "Go on in then."

The officer started to push the door fully open, but in a rare moment of alertness and quick reaction, Joe said, "Please!" and held up his hand to stop that action. "This is a *lady's* room."

"Oh, yeah," the officer said. Then he grinned and added, "Some lady."

Joe's knock was answered by a distant, "*Ja, herein, bitte.*"

The officer looked puzzled, but Joe simply winked at the man and went inside. And Joe thought the wink alone, but certainly together with the knowing little smile that he'd followed it with, was worthy of Humphrey Bogart at his best.

Whether or not Joe's scene was worthy of Hollywood, the one inside the Duke of Windsor suite certainly was. Helga was reclining on the sofa, dressed in something black and slinky—Joe wasn't certain just what it was—that, except for its skin-tight clinginess, appeared modest for Helga. The neckline was cut wide—practically to each shoulder—and low, but not breathtakingly so as was her custom. And a border of white, wispy little feathers along the neckline would have left any but the most searching glance unsatisfied about just how revealing the dress actually was.

Propped languidly on one elbow, a cigarette in a long white holder in her other hand, Helga studied Birnoff an instant before almost whispering in her sexy-husky voice, "Herr Professor, what a surprise. Ah, but you must excuse me." She gestured, to indicate why she did not rise. "Helga is, how do you say, 'below the weather.' The head swims, yes? First Peter's death, then . . . then this crazy police, he makes the crazy accusation."

"Yes," Joe began, blinking rapidly at the erotic vision reclining before him. "I'm certain it's all been quite a shock. I . . . I," Joe sensed he was losing track of what he wanted to say. Maybe if I don't look at her, he thought. So he clasped his hands behind his back and began to pace up and down, studying the floor before him.

"I came to offer my condolences. Over the death of your husband," he said to the floor.

Helga paused in the midst of taking a drag on her cigarette to look quizzically at the professor. "That is . . . good of you," she said.

Joe took a turn and paced back to the point whence he'd just paced forth. "And have they treated you well?" he asked, again seemingly of the floor.

Helga frowned at him, shrugged, and said, "*Ja*. So-so. But the questions. So many questions. Who can all those answers remember?"

That stymied Joe for a moment. He'd had his own list of questions. Should he ask them now, he wondered. He stole a sideways glance at Helga. And he saw her breast swell as she took a long, slow drag on her cigarette. "My word!" he exclaimed softly.

"*Vas ist?*" she quickly asked.

"Oh, nothing. Just nothing." He'd have to be bold, and direct, Joe decided. Otherwise, he'd never get to his reason for coming. So he stretched out his arms, this time extracting real shirt cuffs from a real jacket, and turned to face Helga squarely.

"You didn't kill him, did you?" he asked quickly.

Something like sympathy in his voice muted the bluntness of the question. Helga sensed that—and that she need not be so cautious with Joe as with Parker. She rolled onto her side to face the professor and said, "*Nein*. No."

"Do you have any guesses about who might have?"

"Those crazy art people?" she asked. "Peter was their magazine about to take. Artists, they are all, how else do you say it, crazy, yes?" Here she stopped to point the cigarette at her head and rotate it in a circle. "*Verruckt*, we say in German. Surely it was one of those."

Joe considered this idea a moment before asking, "So, as far as you know, it wasn't Chuck?"

She shrugged. "That, too, would be crazy. He is so, so young. But I was not there. I cannot know."

"You were not there," Joe repeated thoughtfully.

"The door, she was locked. Peter did not answer when I knocked. So I went away."

"You had no key?"

Again she shrugged. "Helga required no key. Peter would always let me in. I came to sunbathe . . . and," here she paused, and a glimmer of brightness or humor passed over her eyes. Then she started over again, but without completing the unfinished thought. "I would every day about noon come to sunbathe, as the sun came onto the balcony. Peter, he would have finished his morning's work and would be ready to depart. So Helga would have the apartment to herself." Again that glimmer of something bright and playful flashed over her eyes.

But Joe didn't see that look. He was comparing what Helga had just said to a list of questions on one of his imagined blackboards in the sky. "Curious," was his only response.

"Yes, so?" Helga asked, still unsure just what to make of her visitor.

Joe resumed his pacing, but he quickly asked, this time of a spot before him in the air instead of the floor, "About that money. The five thousand dollars. I understand your fingerprints were on it."

"Yes, sure. Helga got that money for Peter. He was so busy, yes? So he asked Helga to get the money."

"Often?"

"A few times," she offered with another of her shrugs, and this time one that dropped the neck of her dress halfway down one shoulder. Fortunately, however, Joe was still inspecting the spot before him and didn't see this.

"Curiouser and curiouser," he concluded. Then he caught Helga's perplexed expression and said, "Just an old literary line."

Fourteen

Karl Teasdale thought his strategy was exceedingly clever. It was premised, first, on everything appearing to have occurred by chance. It was just by chance, for example, that he'd wanted to play tennis at all that particular day. Of course, he'd had the courts "staked out" for a day and a half for this opportunity. It was just by chance, as well, that he'd been sitting outside the tennis pro's hut waiting for a singles partner. Of course, he'd actually been sitting there three hours, tying and retying his shoes and checking his other gear. And it was just by chance that he was ready to play when Mary Margaret walked up seeking a pairing herself. What a coincidence!

The second part of Karl's strategy was to let Mary Margaret raise the subject. So he talked of the fine weather, and of her game, and of his problems with his backhand. Anything except *the* subject.

Yet as they neared the end of the set, Karl had begun to fear the strategy would fail him. Mary Margaret had actually seemed a touch shy or ... or something when they'd first met that morning. She hadn't seemed willing to talk at length about anything. But they had, over the course of the play, made *some* progress. They'd talked of the weather between a couple of games. And of her game—which was better than Karl's today. That had been well-complimented by Karl and appropriately pooh-poohed by Mary Margaret, who passed her success off as itself the luck of the day.

The latter compliments, of course, had been difficult for Karl. He was rarely beaten at *his* game by a woman. Yet he attributed it to her relative youth, and to the fact that he was proccupied with thinking about how they would finally get around to *the* subject. His "mental tennis" had to be off as a result of this preoccupation, he told himself.

They'd even discussed his game a bit. He'd broached that subject with a complaint about his backhand today. But before they'd gotten very far into the latter subject, Karl had wanted to drop it himself. He'd suddenly realized it sounded like he was making excuses for losing.

Indeed, things were going badly for his plan as well as his game. But just when Karl was about to despair and do or say something radical, just, in other words, as they had finished their last game and had settled on a courtside bench to rest a moment, Mary Margaret gave him the smallest of openings.

When she'd caught her breath from their last, vigorous rally—which she had won along with the game, set, and match—Mary Margaret admitted, "I have to say, Dr. Teasdale, that you've really been most gracious today."

"Please, I thought we'd graduated long ago to a first-name basis," he pleaded. "I'm not *that* old." But Karl held back the thought: do I suppose she means I've been a gracious loser?

"Oh, of course. It's just that I've felt sort of embarrassed. And it was so kind of you not to bring the subject up."

Now Karl was really worried. Maybe she didn't want to talk about the murder. But her next remark ended his concern.

"Yes, I fear I was an awful hostess the other night. Getting drunk and all."

Karl was caught off his guard by the admission, but he thought his recovery a rapid one. "Oh, that. I really thought nothing of it. I was a touch inebriated myself."

"It's been all the stress of this . . . this murder. Then, when Calvin pulled off his little *coup* by buying out some of the other partners—and when he wanted to celebrate—well, I'm afraid I just let myself go too far."

True enough, it was a very tiny opening, but Karl figured he'd better plunge into it. This might be the best he'd get. So he picked up his tennis racket and sighted down its length, pretending to check for a warp. And he said, as indifferently as he could manage, "Yes, I can understand the strain you've been under. This murder's been hard on everyone here. Everybody's off his game, so to speak."

"That's just the way I feel," Mary Margaret admitted. "In spite of that man's . . . I guess you could say 'nastiness,' he didn't deserve to be murdered. And the murder alone, that would have been unsettling enough for us all. But, then, to have your friends and . . . and, well, to have your friends and even you yourself become the suspects. It's all been a great deal to bear. I'm just so glad they've caught the guilty ones."

"They have?" Karl thought his feigned surprise a triumph.

"Oh, yes. Haven't you heard? It's been all over the hotel. It was his wife, that cheap looking porno star. And that cute young tennis assistant. What was his name? She probably led the poor boy on, so he'd do the dirty work. I bet she'll inherit millions, too."

"Who'd have thought it?"

"I'm just glad it's over."

"Yes, I guess that means that, as you put it, you and your friends, have been cleared of suspicion."

For the first time today Mary Margaret laughed, and she replied, "And what's even better, Cal and I have stopped being suspicious of each other."

In a flash Karl knew just what to do. He dropped his racket and turned to stare at Mary Margaret, his eyes opened to their widest. "You can't possibly mean!" was all he said.

"Yes," she laughed again. "Cal feared I had done it. To protect Mrs. Bertram from the hurt and shame of losing the magazine. And I'm afraid I suspected Cal might have done it to protect Mrs. Bertram in order to keep me happy."

After a moment's pause and reflection, she added, "You saw the way Cal acted the other night at dinner. Remember, when poor Professor Birnoff made that innocent remark that even Cal or I could have been the murderer."

"That did seem to inflame him."

"Just like a man. He thought I might have been the murderer, but he also thought he could play the big, protective male to shield me." She shook her head, and her all-knowing smile suggested the usual judgment of womankind on mankind.

In light of their progress so far, Karl decided his strategy was working well enough to give it the ultimate test. So he began to pack his gear into his bag and, once again assuming his indifferent pose of offering conversation for the sake of politeness, he said, "Too bad you had to go through that. I'm surprised your alibis didn't eliminate the need for it."

"That's actually why Cal suspected, or feared, at first, that it might have been me. He didn't think I had an alibi."

"And did you?"

"It turns out I did, but at the time I wasn't certain myself. That's because I didn't hear for a couple of days the approximate time that Halsey was murdered. I think that sheriff's detective was purposefully secretive about some things like that to keep us all in the dark. But, what happened, you see, was that I'd come back from Sand Key on the hotel launch late that morning. Walking back to the hotel, I was in such pain from my sunburn that I stopped along the path to apply more ointment. And this nice lady from Vermont, another guest at the hotel, stopped to help. She sprayed it on my back for me. Then we fell to chatting about sunburn remedies. We talked so long, when I realized how late it was, I had to hurry back to the hotel. I feared I wouldn't be able to change in time to get to the afternoon business meeting. But that woman and the time I spent with her turn out to cover me for the time they think Halsey was killed."

"As if anyone could have realistically suspected you in the first place. But, then, I guess you could be scolded, too, for being suspicious of your husband."

"Now, of course, I know you're right. But Cal works in a very rough and, at times, very violent business. I hate to say it, but I believe him capable of doing it. And, besides, he started acting rather odd almost as soon as we heard of Halsey's death."

"Odd? How so?"

"He became very preoccupied. He made some secretive phone calls and slipped off for some private meetings here in the hotel. Later, I learned he'd simply called his banker and had been meeting with Aaron Farfel, plotting how he'd buy out the other partners. Men are rather silly at times, aren't they, Professor?"

Mary Margaret was struck—as soon as she'd asked it—by how foolish the question was when asked of a man. So she laughed again and explained, "I mean, there Calvin was sneaking around like a criminal to plot some minor business deal."

"But at least he wasn't a criminal after all, eh?" Karl probed again.

"No, because he had an alibi, too. I think he'd just held it back in the hope that suspicion of him might divert any from me. Men! Oh, once again, Dr. Teasdale, present company excepted."

"My sex is certainly taking a drubbing today. I will defer my rebuttal on the shortcomings of the opposite, supposedly fairer and weaker, but I suspect only more sharp-tongued, sex. But in recognition of my forbearance, satisfy my curiosity and tell me Calvin's alibi."

Mary Margaret beamed mischievously at him and said, "His boots!"

"What?"

"His boots. His thousand-dollar alligator boots. He'd worn them that morning, forgetting he was going out with Halsey on one of the hotel's boats after lunch. And I'm thankful Halsey didn't get to keep that date. I'm still suspicious of Calvin's motives and intentions for that little rendezvous.

"But, you see, when Cal went to the dock to rent the boat, he looked down and saw he had on his favorite—and most

142

expensive—boots. Now, no Texan, even one as rich as my husband, is going to risk getting his alligator boots wet. So he walked back to the hotel to change. And it seems the maid was there cleaning the room when he arrived. He ended up chatting with her long enough to preclude his being able to get to Halsey's apartment in time to be the killer."

"Well, I'm certainly glad to hear that," Karl concluded.

*   *   *

If Joe Birnoff had been the type to use a little casual profanity, now would have been the time. Instead, he saw the humor in the situation and smiled at his predicament. He stood, alone and entirely perplexed, in a long hall of offices in the administrative wing of the hotel. It was late, long after his dinner with Karl. And the hall along with its various offices was dark and apparently empty. But Joe knew he must be right. Parker must be here in his little office. The only problem was, Joe'd forgotten just which office that was.

Joe had started his postdinner stroll a few minutes ago, and he'd seen the Sheriff's Department cruiser as soon as he stepped out the front door of the hotel. He guessed immediately that it was Parker, but the desk clerk had been no help in finding the man. In fact, the desk was momentarily unmanned or, as Joe attempted to remember to say to his verbally trendy colleagues, in spite of its vulgar sound, "unpersoned."

Anyway, Joe had assumed Parker had gone to the office. It was far too late to be interviewing witnesses or suspects. So here Joe was, fussing along the hall, talking to himself, and gingerly trying one door knob after another in hopes of finding the right one.

Six doors in a row had been locked. But at the seventh Joe was successful. His slow, hesitant twist of the knob had produced a satisfying click, and the door had yielded a fraction. He eased it open a couple of inches and, bent half over, peered cautiously into the dim room.

There, sitting alone at the small desk, in the glow of a

single feeble lamp, was Detective Parker. And Parker, too, was leaning forward, staring intently at the door in anticipation of whoever was making this surreptitious entrance.

"Hell, Professor!" the officer said with some relief. "I thought I had a cat burglar on my hands, as well."

Joe opened the door, stood up, and grinned. "Nobody here but us insomnious professors," he said. "May I come in?"

Parker waved grandly at the spartan room. "My place," he offered, "is yours. I'd offer some coffee, too, but I'm afraid I've about finished my *mocha U'Totem.*" He nodded to a styrofoam cup on the desk.

Joe had advanced to the desk for a quick look at whatever items of interest it might bear in public view. He'd learned to do that every time he had an appointment with his dean at Oberlin. That stratagem, along with an ability to read print upside-down, had kept him in on juicy campus gossip.

But there was not much of interest here tonight: Parker's coffee cup and a big ring of keys. And his feet. Yes, the most interesting things on the desk were Parker's stockinged feet, propped up there as he leaned back in his chair. Joe Birnoff liked that. A man who relaxes with his shoes off, thought Joe, is my kind of person. Joe was certain from his own experience that it did something positive for the brain, who knows, maybe even for the cardiovascular system itself, to sit awhile and relax with one's feet up like that.

"You, eh, working late?" Joe ventured.

"Just thinking about some loose ends."

Joe was inspecting the desk itself now, searching with his fingertips the depths of some of the more prominent scars on its battered surface. "I must say, I'm surprised there are any. Loose ends, that is. You certainly tied everything in a neat little package the other day when you explained it to Karl and me."

"Neat packages sometimes have a way of unraveling on you."

Joe looked up in surprise to ask, "Is that happening with this one?"

144

The detective took a long time to answer. "Let's just say it's not developed exactly like I thought. It's just . . ." Parker stopped. He looked in the now-empty coffee cup and frowned. Then he admitted, "All right, so there are some problems with the love triangle thing. I know there's some odd bits of evidence. Still, I've turned it every different way in my mind, and that still comes out the best explanation."

Joe cleared his throat and began, "I wonder if I might suggest—"

But Parker stopped him with a raised hand. "I don't know, Professor. Not tonight. I don't think I'm good for any more."

"Any more what?"

"Economics. Your buddy Teasdale's been in here three times in the last couple of days, drawing curves and diagrams all over that blackboard and giving me all kinds of economics lectures on how to solve this crime. I've seen so many of those damn curves, I get like carsick when I just think about them."

Joe turned to study the blackboard and its collection of graphs and curves—some half-erased, some squeezed in at odd angles in odd corners, and some drawn on top of others. "Yes," Joe said, "I believe I see Karl's work—and his thinking—here."

But Parker was not really listening. He shook his head and parroted, "We move *up* this curve and *along* this other one, and further out this set of curves. And where these two curves intersect, we blah, blah, blah. Up a curve, down a curve, around a curve. Hell, I see those things in my sleep now. They're like fog-shrouded hills and valleys or, like they say in the storybooks, hills and dales. And just like in the storybooks, in my dreams they're hills and dales harboring secret, important meaning. And in my dreams I'm groping to see them through the fog and to puzzle out their meaning, as if once I do, I'll be able to solve this murder."

Joe's eyes widened in response to this little speech. He smiled, and then he said, "Why that's perfectly marvelous, Detective Parker. 'Fog-shrouded hills and dales of wisdom whose meaning is difficult to discern.' I wish I'd had a tape recorder to capture that for posterity. And I must say, the analogy is entirely fitting. I often suspect that's about how my students feel when I start my lectures on business cycles. But you, at least, recognize there is wisdom in those hills and dales, as you call them. Universal wisdom, universal like lines carved in old hewed stone. And whose meaning, once understood, would make the solution to this puzzle as clear as a spring-fed lake."

Parker shook his head and concluded, "Maybe so, but right now everything looks as murky as convenience store coffee."

"Small wonder," Joe agreed, studying again the scribbling on Parker's blackboard. "It does appear to be a complicated case, at least to my novice's eye. And, I daresay my colleague has complicated more than simplified matters for you. You say he was here *three* times?"

"It seemed like a hundred."

"Yes, he's clearly violated Birnoff's First Law: A little economics goes a long way."

"Yeah, I don't think he knows that one." Parker shook his head and frowned at the bare desk, perhaps indicating it had as much meaning for him as did the cluttered blackboard.

"Odd you should mention the murkiness of this crime, however," Joe said. "That's something of the way I've seen it, too. It's like there's too much there. I'm having problems sorting out what's important. And there are a couple of specific points about which I'm especially uncertain."

"Only a couple?" Parker laughed, but with little humor.

"Yes, mostly about things you said the other day and that I've forgotten. I really should jot more things down. But I seem to have lost my notepad. Can't for the life of me remember where I last used it. Maybe it was—"

"Professor!"

"Yes?"

"Those murky points?"

"Oh, yes. Sorry. Let me see now. Oh, indeed. About this fight Halsey had with his, uh, assailant, if you'll accept that word. Was he beaten around much from it? Bruised? Battered? That sort of thing."

Parker thought a minute and then said, "Hard to tell. The fall from the balcony did a lot of damage. He tore his leg on the broken railing as he went over. He got scratched and bruised by that tree he fell through. And then hitting the old concrete from five floors up—well, that had just about the results you'd expect. So some wounds he might of had from the fight would've been covered by the ones from the fall."

"But did you find anything like fingernail scratches, gouges on his face or arms, or any similar wounds from the fight?"

"Only a few day-old ones. They were from the fight with Farfel, as we understand."

"How about anything else? Any unusual odors or . . . perfumes on the body?"

Parker laughed. "What are you thinking, Professor? He rolled around on the floor fighting with the murderer and got their Chanel No. 5, or their Brut, all over his body?"

"Perhaps," was Joe's wounded reply.

"Sorry. There was nothing like that."

Joe paced the room slowly, thinking this over. He walked to the blackboard and appeared to be searching it intently. Wrinkling his brow, he started to ask a question. But he did not, for suddenly he knew the answer. There was no chalk with which he could draw his own diagram because Parker had taken it away. Now he wouldn't have to endure any more of Karl's—or Joe's—visual aids.

"One other thing," Joe began.

"Sure, why not."

"I'm confused about Halsey's movements that morning. In and out of the apartment."

"Oh, yeah. That's part of the clincher. He arrived, uh, when was it? I guess about nine-thirty or ten. *My* notebook's locked in my car. The maid saw him and he even said 'top of the morning' or something cheery like that to her. Crazy Brits! Then later, about eleven thirty or so, he left. And luckily the maid saw him that time, too. I figure that's when he was leaving, according to his usual custom, knowing he'd sneak back later and catch his wife and the kid in the sack together."

"So the maid's certain about the time?"

"Pretty much. They talked a couple of minutes about how he wanted the apartment cleaned."

"Hadn't she done it yet?"

"Oh, sure. At least as Halsey wanted it that morning. He wouldn't let her clean the whole place. Claimed he was preparing the most important business pitch of his trip and she'd bother him too much. So he let her change the sheets and towels. And he requested, as usual, extra towels. Helga used them to cover that balcony railing when she sunbathed, remember? Although I'm surprised she bothered."

"So why'd they talk more about it? Cleaning the room, that is."

"Halsey was telling the maid she could give the place a good going over the next day, because his business would be finished."

"If only he'd known how right he was," Joe concluded.

Fifteen

"I believe, Professor," Mrs. Bertram was saying to Joe, "that I understand entirely Aaron's weaknesses as well as his strengths. Aaron is often rude and ill-mannered. His taste in clothing is ghastly, and he associates with an unfortunate class of people. Yet his knowledge of art is immense, and his judgment about currents in the art world entirely infallible. It is fair to say, of course, that he has no head for business. Yet no one else, I am entirely convinced, could have achieved as much with *Artworld* as he."

"So you don't blame him for Halsey's takeover attempt?" Joe asked.

"Blame him? I hardly see why I should."

"It was his poor head for business, so to speak, and its attendant financial losses which made the other partners sympathetic to Halsey's offer."

"My word, and you an economist!" Mrs. Bertram almost scolded. "I hardly blame Aaron. He was simply doing what I told him to do from the beginning: make the magazine the best of its kind in the world. Besides, our business may be art, but it's still business. And you, Professor, should know particularly well that takeover efforts like this are an everyday part of business today."

Her little lecture ended, Mrs. Bertram took up her cup for another sip of tea. And Joe Birnoff, behind his vacant smile, was thinking, this is one tough business woman. Or should

I say, "business person"? He pondered the question a moment but came to no conclusion. Since he had other matters in his head and since those matters were quite important ones, Joe came back mentally to Mrs. Bertram.

He blinked a few times and shifted in his chair. The two of them were having afternoon tea on one of the hotel's verandas, and Joe would have to admit, at least to himself, that he had used his friend Karl's idea of a clever way to engage his quarry to get this interview. He had walked up to her table and asked straightaway whether he could join her for tea. Once he was ensconced at the table, the subjects of the magazine and the murder had come up naturally.

Now, Joe decided, it was time to move toward what he'd come to learn. He took a sip of his own tea and then said, "Perhaps such things as takeover attempts are an everyday part of business. But most businesses that are the subjects of such efforts—even if they resist the effort successfully—usually go through quite a bit of difficulty in doing so."

"I do not mean to belittle the ways it affected Arsgratia. Why, we practically had partners fighting each other at some of our meetings. Poor Aaron was shattered. I fear I'll have to pack him off to London or Paris a week for recuperative purposes. And, well, even I myself, I was quite disturbed at first."

"I must say," Joe put in, "and I mean it as a compliment, that you appeared far less disturbed than many of the others."

"Though I hate to admit it, that's probably a benefit of age and experience. I simply resolved to do the best I could to defeat Halsey. And, were I to fail, I knew what I must do in that instance, as well."

Joe's mental ears perked up at this firm pronouncement. "Oh, do tell me your strategy," he fairly bubbled. "It sounds like a terrific 'case study,' as we call them."

"I made the best argument against Halsey that I could in the private meetings of the shareholders. You may remember that you and I discussed those matters. I used some of your ideas, in fact."

150

Joe smiled with pride.

"They did fail, however," Mrs. Bertram added, and Joe's smile turned from a proud to a bittersweet one.

The woman saw his reaction and quickly went on, "The fault, Professor, was hardly in our arguments. It was, I fear, the audience at which they were directed. The thought of a fattened bank account was too powerful against what I could offer as an alternative."

"So you lost that round," Joe concluded.

She nodded, but with a firmness that suggested no remorse.

"And what was, or was to have been, your strategy in the next round?"

"I went straight to the devil himself. It was on the very morning he was killed. Detective Parker tells me that I may have been the last person—save the murderer, of course—to see him alive."

"You were going to bargain with Halsey?" Joe was intrigued by this information.

"It was my intention. Yet that failed, too."

"And what bargain did you offer him?"

"My first offer was to strike a deal, repugnant as that would have been. I told him I wouldn't resist his effort to buy into Arsgratia. And I had some ideas—some concessions on my part—about how we could alter the format and marketing of the magazine. Frankly, that was a distasteful thing, but I felt I must attempt it to save some of the reputation of the magazine."

"I infer he wouldn't bargain."

"That's correct. In fact, he'd hardly even listen to my proposal. Not even to my second one, which was greatly in his favor."

"You had a second one?"

"Yes. If he didn't accept the first one, I was prepared to sell him my controlling interest in Arsgratia on the spot."

"You were!" Joe was astounded. "You'd have sold out entirely?"

"As I indicated earlier, this *is* business, Professor Birnoff.

151

I had lost the fight to save *Artworld*, so it was time to pull out what financial resources I could and move on."

"But what would you have done? If you'd sold out like that?"

"Done? Why there was only one thing to be done. I'd start all over again with a new magazine. It was quite clear that *Artworld* under Halsey's leadership would not continue to serve its serious art clientele. And those were the people I wanted to serve. So I would simply have started another magazine to do so. In fact, when I left Halsey—after he turned me down—I went in search of Aaron to start planning that very effort. I was going to lose *Artworld*, so I had to think about the future. I searched the hotel and eventually found Aaron at the dining room shortly before noon. We discussed my plans and would have begun working on them that same afternoon, but then word of Halsey's death came."

"Amazing," was all Joe could say. His mind was spinning off on four or five separate tracks simultaneously. He must have played out each of these lines of thought a bit, for he was lost to his companion a good minute or so, but then he floated back to reality to muse, "It does seem surprising he didn't take your second offer."

"In truth, I don't even think he considered it. He seemed, well, preoccupied. And perhaps annoyed that he had to talk to me at all. I was quite offended by his behavior."

"Preoccupied," Joe repeated. "Yes, I suppose he would have been."

*　　*　　*

"I tell you," Joe was saying to Karl, "he's been spending a lot of time in that little office they gave him here at the hotel. Let's just check there first."

The two professors had been out walking—discussing what they now knew of Halsey's death. But they had concluded both the walk and the discussion and were heading back to the hotel. Just now they were crossing the sun-bathing and bar area around the pool.

Their passage did not go unnoticed, however, for Calvin Caldwell—sitting at a table having drinks with his wife and Aaron Farfel—glanced up and saw them. "Look," he laughed to his companions, "there go the 'Bob and Ray' of the economics world. Watch me get them going."

"Oh, Cal," Mary Margaret sighed. "Must you?" And Aaron mumbled, "I think I've got to be someplace else right away, any place else."

But Caldwell had to have his sport. He motioned for Aaron to stay in his seat, whispered, "Just watch," and then hailed the professors. After one of those surprised "who us?" reactions, the two men came over to the table.

"Care to join us?" Calvin offered. "You might even find our subject of interest. We're plotting how to refinance some of Arsgratia's existing debt under more favorable terms, so we can go out and borrow more money."

"I suppose the practical businessman's view of such matters might be of at least modest interest," Karl responded, trying to hide for Mary Margaret's sake his dislike of her husband. "So tell us," Karl went on, "just what are your plans?"

Caldwell, however, had another conversational tack in mind, for he shook his head and then lamented—with a gravity that surprised both his wife and Aaron, "We're just trying to get together a reasonable amount of operating capital. It's too bad we can't be like the damned federal government and just borrow whatever we want whenever we want. Hell, anybody could be successful in private business if they didn't have to be concerned with their debts."

That remark had its intended effect on both professors, although their reactions were quite different.

"The government, too," Joe said defensively, "although it is admittedly you and I who constitute 'the government' in these terms, also has to be concerned with its debt. And in spite of what you may think, that debt will eventually be paid."

153

"Yet the question of whether the public debt must be eventually paid is hardly the most important one," Karl put in. "As my colleague here suggests, it will be paid. In fact, the government is borrowing money almost daily to refinance its debt. What are important, and what Joe is not so ready to agree with me about, are the sacrifices and costs associated with persistent government deficits."

"Yeah, like when some politician finally has the guts to raise my taxes even higher, is that it, in order to reduce the deficit?" Calvin prompted.

"It is far more than that," Karl replied. "As I would have hoped any practical businessman would have known. You said a moment ago that you plan for Arsgratia to borrow more money for operating capital. Yet because of our large public debt, the company will pay an interest rate on that borrowing that is higher than it otherwise would be."

Mary Margaret was puzzled. "Wait a minute. I thought we were talking about the government's debt and our taxes. You lost me when you jumped to interest rates."

Karl sighed. He liked this woman, so he tried to be patient. "When the government runs a deficit," he began slowly, "it finances that deficit—the public spending which is not covered by available revenues—with borrowing from the private sector. Since the government must do this to pay its current bills, it competes with private individuals and companies who also are seeking money to borrow. This competition, or heightened demand, for funds causes the interest rate to rise. A simple supply-and-demand situation, right? The result is that some private borrowers are crowded out of the market—they can't afford to borrow at the higher rates—and those who do get funds pay higher interest rates on them than they otherwise would."

"My, those deficits are even worse than I'd imagined," Mary Margaret concluded.

Karl beamed. But at the same time he looked across the table and saw that Joe was frowning at this argument and at Karl's success in impressing their audience with it. Joe's as-

154

sorted bodily twitches and facial expressions told Karl, as well, that his friend was about to object.

"My colleague," Karl whispered in an aside to Mary Margaret, "is about to take issue with me. Probably over my 'crowding out' argument."

And sure enough, Joe's rebuttal was immediately forthcoming. "I do hope," he began, "that you'll consider an alternative to Professor Teasdale's position. He voices the usual monetarist line. We Keynesians, while accepting that some crowding out may occur, believe that it does not occur to any large degree. In economic downturns some funds are typically idle, that is, are not loaned out, so government borrowing must exhaust those idle funds before anyone is crowded out of the market."

Karl smiled at Mary Margaret before saying, "My colleague missed the most basic point. It makes little difference whether the deficit is covered by borrowing or eliminated by raising taxes. The deficit is not itself the problem. Excessive government spending is the problem. It crowds out private spending. I stick by my scholarly guns—and they are big 'guns,' by the way, within the economics profession—on that point. And as far as idle funds just lying around is concerned, well, efficient financial markets should prohibit that."

Joe was now quite visibly disturbed. Yet their host, for his part, appeared to be enjoying himself enormously. And he decided to push the argument along a little further by asking of Karl, "It sounds like you believe, just like I do, that this government budget is really a mess."

"But of course. Yet, as I said, it's not the deficit *per se*, but the high level of government spending that concerns me."

"And you, Professor Birnoff—" Calvin tried to ask. But the Texan had already created more momentum than he knew, and Karl cut the man off in mid-sentence to pronounce, "I can tell you exactly what he'll say. It's the tired, old Keynesian line: We shouldn't worry too much about the deficit. The government can safely run deficits in the short run just so over the long run it's in balance during periods of high employment.

155

And he'd probably add that, in exchange for any given year's deficit, we get all those nifty government programs that he and his liberal friends value so highly. Lots of wonderful public services instead of the private goods we'd have if government wasn't spending so heavily."

"Right, just like all that defense spending you and your conservative friends value so highly," Joe blurted out. "And, like most of your monetarist associates you're amazingly insensitive to my long-run argument about deficits, the one that you yourself just summarized."

"Your long-run view! Now that is a laugher!" Karl shot back. "A Keynesian arguing a long-run position is certainly ironic given Lord John Maynard's view on the long run. I like to think that if Keynes could have known our economic circumstances today, his dictum would have been: 'In the long run, we're all monetarists.'"

Karl crossed his arms in smug self-satisfaction, while Joe bristled all the more. But Calvin didn't want them to slacken their pace, so he quickly asked of Karl, "Just what are those bad consequences of dealing with the deficit that you mentioned?"

"They arise because the Federal Reserve System is forced to monetize the debt, that is, to turn it into a larger volume of money in the economy, to counter the upward pressure on interest rates created by all that government borrowing."

"The Federal Reserve!" Mary Margaret said in exasperation. "This deficit problem gets more complicated all the time."

"Yes, it's ever so fascinating, isn't it?" Aaron sighed.

"It's really quite simple," Karl went on undeterred. "When the Treasury has to borrow a lot of money to cover the government's bills, it pushes up the interest rate, as I said. But the Federal Reserve then has to buy government securities in the financial markets in order to provide banks with more funds, in order to get the banks to lend more money, in order to offset, at least in part, the additional demand for loans created by the deficit."

156

"In order to confuse us even further," Aaron said wearily.

"I know where you're going with this," Joe countered. "But you—"

"Stop!" Karl interrupted. "I know your rebuttal, as well. When will you accept the fact that we can't keep inflating the money supply in this way? You know that research has shown the supply of money influences the Gross National Product in the short run and prices and hence inflation in the long run."

"But you know the counter research that argues that the role of money, while important, is not so pervasive," Joe offered more confidently, now beginning to see his own argumentative path more clearly. "Besides, your position assumes that the private sector is inherently stable and that these government actions are upsetting that stability."

"Precisely!" Karl shouted, leaning over the table now in his enthusiasm. "I'm glad you recognize my position. I suppose you still cling to your outmoded, born-of-the-Great-Depression view that the private sector is *not* inherently stable. That we must control aggregate economic demand and hence the state of the economy by manipulating government taxing and spending. The old Keynesian fiscal policy."

"But of course."

"Then why, might I ask, have the government's taxing and spending policies not been successful, especially of late, in achieving those economic goals?"

Now Joe was really mad. He puffed up like a balloon and flapped his arms and rolled his eyes in exasperation as if to indicate, I'm arguing with an idiot. Then he leaned over the table toward his friend to say, "Surely you know the difference between valid theory on the one hand and improper implementation on the other. Wait!" Here Joe held up *his* hand, stopping Karl from interrupting again.

"I know what *you're* going to say," Joe went on. "If only **we** could throw off this miserable fiscal policy which never works. And I know, as well," Joe continued, "you're going to say that, if only we had instead the simple policy of controlling the rate of increase of the money supply, assuming its inherent stabilizing influence on the private sector, then, you'd say, we would stabilize both prices and long-term growth."

"You *do* understand it after all!" Karl responded in mock triumph.

"As if political considerations wouldn't influence the implementation of that approach if it were our primary economic policy!" Joe shot back. "How politically naive of you. Just let me put it a way that even a layperson here—" Joe turned to gesture to Calvin and stopped in mid-sentence. He blinked and, after an instant, slowly closed his mouth.

Karl looked around in surprise, too. They were alone. The others had fled in the heat of the argument.

"I surmise," Joe concluded, "they they really didn't want to hear about the deficit tonight. Ah, well, another time perhaps. Now what was it we were doing before we met them anyway?"

"Going to look for Detective Parker," Karl reminded him with a touch of frustration.

"Oh, yes. Of course."

Sixteen

"Well, everyone's here now," Detective Parker announced a touch impatiently.

Joe Birnoff, standing in the balcony doorway, deep in thought and with his hands clasped behind his back, turned to confirm this statement. Owl-eyed, he surveyed the party. And yes, everyone *was* there.

Parker was by the door, ready, Joe supposed, to catch the murderer should he—or she—attempt to flee. Mrs. Bertram sat, poised and calm, on one sofa. Alongside her was Mary Margaret, ever the eager pupil. And Calvin sat on the sofa-arm by his wife, smiling something of a what-kind-of-a-corny-stunt-is-this smile.

On the other sofa Helga sat alone. She looked, as she always did, charged with erotic electricity, the energy of which was barely contained below her sultry-sulky exterior. But Helga also looked nervous. Joe could see it in her eyes. She kept looking around the room, from one person to another, as if probing for the tiniest hint of explanation for what must have appeared a strange, foreign ritual.

There were two other nervous people in the room, as well. Chuck, the hero of tennis court and mattress, lover of the rich lord's wife, accused of adultery, blackmail, murder, and no doubt a few other devious deeds, was one of these. Poor Chuck, looking like a sheepish adolescent caught in the cookie jar, stood in a corner across the room, as far away from everyone else as he could get. Embarrassed, he avoided everyone else's eyes. It was as if the unmasking of his sexual exploits had left him physically naked, as well, in the presence of these other people. He turned and fidgeted, uncomfortable now for his public exposure.

And there was Aaron. In his rumpled suit and with his rumpled, New-York-coarse manner Aaron ran one hand across his head and patted at his thinning, curly mass of hair as if trying to get it in just the right tangled disarray. And he kept fingering the spectacles that hung on a cord around his neck.

Finally, there was Karl. Karl looked as impatient as Detective Parker. Had Joe remembered, he would have known Karl had a tennis date in half an hour with a stockbroker he'd met at breakfast. In confirmation of his impatience, Karl cleared his throat and said to his friend, "Indeed, everyone's here now."

"Indeed," Joe repeated. "Shall I begin?" he asked of Karl.

Karl nodded.

"You're certain you don't want to do it?" Joe asked. "I really wouldn't mind."

"Joe!" Karl said sternly.

"Yes, yes. Just as long as you don't mind." Then Joe turned to the assembled group before him and said, "We, Karl and I, are pleased that you agreed to come. And that Detective Parker made this little demonstration possible. It seemed particularly fitting, too, that we return to the scene of the crime." Here Joe raised one arm to gesture to the room, which was Halsey's condominium apartment.

But no one reacted to this gesture, so Joe mumbled, "Yes, so here we are." Then his eyes brightened and he added, "Karl and I have asked you here because we wish to, in fact we will, explicate for you the circumstances of Lord Halsey's death."

Several heads, previously only vaguely attentive to the professor, now turned to fix on him.

"And the, shall we say, 'culprit,' in his death will be exposed," Joe added.

A few hearts might have skipped a beat over that line.

Joe sensed the reactions around him and, while obviously proud to have been their cause, he also felt the need for self-effacement. "Of course, we really owe most of it to what we learned from the eminent detective here," Joe explained, nodding toward Parker. "In the beginning, what thoughts we had were so ill-formed that one shouldn't dignify them by the label of hypotheses, much less theories."

"I believe," Karl had to say, "that I offered a relatively explicit set of hypotheses quite early. And I believe—"

"Oh," Joe interrupted him. "So you *do* want to explain it."

Karl fumed, but he controlled his temper and said carefully, "No, in truth I just want you to get on with it."

"Yes, yes. No embellishment then. I'll go straight to the heart of it."

Karl cast an expression of thanks toward the heavens as his friend began to pace and talk, or rather, to lecture.

"Solving a crime like this one," Joe began, "I've come to decide, is much like seeking an explanation in one's research for some economic circumstance. Both depend upon the use of the scientific method. Not just scientific tools, mind you, things like fingerprinting, medical autopsies, and such. Instead they depend on the scientific method for seeking explanations for given phenomena.

"In both instances we observe a set of facts we wish to explain. In the one case it might be some common form of economic behavior. Potential buyers of a certain good, for example, might characteristically respond in a certain way in a certain set of circumstances. And we wish to know why.

"In the other case we find a body and a collection of evidence at the scene that suggests murder. And we wish to know 'who dun it?'

"Now in both cases we begin by considering the various alternative answers, for usually there are several competing hypotheses which might explain the economic behavior we have observed in the first case, just as there often are several suspects who might have been the murderer in the second. Each suspect, you see, is analogous to a separate hypothesis.

"Thus, in the case of the murder, we wish to determine the one suspect who has a plausible motive, who has no credible alibi, and against whom the available evidence is most compelling.

"Now, I believe everyone here, save Karl and me, of course, had a plausible motive for the crime. Karl would also say each of those was an economic motive, at least in part. Now we could review each suspect—or hypothesis—in turn and in detail. As it happens, however, Detective Parker made it possible early on virtually to rule out some of the suspects."

Parker raised his eyebrows here and Joe turned to say to him directly, "It was in our first private meeting with you. You told us it would have required a man's strength—pushing against it or pushing someone else against it—to have broken that balcony railing. The female suspects, in all due respect to society's current re-evaluation of what was once pejoratively called the 'weaker sex,' appear exonerated by that fact." Here Joe nodded to the three women on the sofas.

"You also quickly provided a possible solution with the 'Chuck and Helga' explanation," Joe went on to Parker. "But Karl and I sensed a problem with that because of the Prisoner's Dilemma we later explained to you."

And for the rest of the group, Karl put in, "Neither of them would plead guilty to a lesser charge when the other might have done so, leaving the first one to take the major guilt and punishment."

"We were led to seek an alternative explanation," Joe went on. "Yet we quickly eliminated the remaining male suspects, as well. Calvin first, owing to his Texan's sartorial fastidiousness."

Caldwell nearly slipped off the sofa-arm in surprise as he asked, "My what?"

"Your boots," Joe explained. "When you returned to your room to change your boots, the maid was working there and can verify the time.

"Aaron, likewise, is eliminated because of the time when he met Mrs. Bertram at the dining room. He was vague about the hour. Remember, Detective Parker, that was the point you wanted to illustrate when you read his statement to us. But Mrs. Bertram knew it to be just before noon. And the luncheon hostess, by the way, confirms that."

This last comment induced Parker to raise his eyebrows for further explanation. "The lady recalled very vividly Aaron's, uh, attire," Joe explained.

"But who's left, then?" Mary Margaret suddenly blurted out. "You've accounted for the men. Unless . . . ," her voice trailed off, but she shot a glance at the nervous Chuck across the room.

"It could possibly have been a woman, maybe by sheer luck or by accident," Joe admitted with a frown of annoyance. Yet he was unwilling to deviate from the intended outline of his little lecture, so he added. "But, alas . . . oh, I suppose I should say 'fortunately,' it appears it was not a woman. Mrs. Bertram and Mary Margaret both have alibis— Mrs. Bertram because she was with Aaron so soon after she left Halsey's apartment and Mary Margaret by the word of another guest she met returning from the boat launch."

"Hell, you smart guys have eliminated everybody," Calvin interjected. "Unless you're not as smart as you think. You've explained solid alibis for everybody except Parker's original suspects. That stuff about not pleading guilty doesn't sound so convincing to me, anyway."

Helga flinched at this remark, and the fidgety Chuck mumbled something to himself in his nervousness.

Joe smiled at this interruption and observed to Karl, "The practical man of business is not satisfied by mere theory."

Then, to the entire group, Joe said, "Let me continue, for there is much more. Karl and I, at least, found the evidence so far compelling. But the crime remained unsolved, and there were some quite puzzling aspects to it.

"First, there were the clues: this room in disarray from a fight, the money in the envelopes, the notes to Chuck and Helga, the towels on the balcony. Such a lot of clues! Too many clues, Karl and I thought.

"And there was one person who had no alibi, although that person tried at length to create one. And further, that person's behavior was very suspicious. Suspicious in a way that led us to see what was wrong with all those clues." Joe paused and his audience leaned forward in anticipation.

"The clues explain," he went on, "why the wrong person, so to speak, died."

"The wrong person!" Parker exclaimed.

"The evidence," Joe asked of the detective, "who does the evidence suggest was in this room the morning of the crime?"

"Why, Halsey and Helga and Chuck and . . . and Mrs. Bertram."

"It looked like Helga had started sunbathing, Chuck had joined her, and Halsey had caught them together, right?" Joe asked.

"That's right."

"Yet I submit something quite different happened. Which person in this scenario went to elaborate lengths to ensure an alibi for coming and going to the apartment?"

"Why . . . ," Parker could not say.

"It was Halsey," Joe said flatly. "By going out of his way to talk to the maid on the floor both times."

Joe let this sink in before adding, "And yet when Halsey came back—presumably coming secretively by the stairs—no one saw him.

"Who," Joe now asked pointedly of Mrs. Bertram, "was nervous and preoccupied that morning? So preoccupied that he failed to seize an offer that would have given him control of Arsgratia in a single transaction?"

Mrs. Bertram's eyes grew wide.

"Yes, it was Halsey," Joe answered for her.

Turning back to Parker, the professor asked, "And who kept the maid from cleaning this room that morning? Kept her out so that Chuck's and Helga's fingerprints—from the prior day's assignation—would not be cleaned away?"

They were all stunned. Even Calvin Caldwell was clearly surprised. But Chuck and Helga, the two accused conspirators, were especially fixed on Joe. The professor beamed with pleasure, and his pausing to enjoy their surprise induced Karl to pick up the story.

"I believe, that is, we believe," Karl said, "that Halsey planned to murder Helga here, because of her infidelities. He probably feared the cost of divorce. It might have destroyed his financial empire. So he planned a complicated trap. He knew his wife's, and Chuck's, usual arrival times after he'd left the apartment each day.

"So he first planted those notes in Chuck's locker and in Helga's room. Then, on the fateful morning and after his appointment with Mrs. Bertram, he left by the elevator, first making sure to talk to the maid so she could verify the time. Then he slipped back up the stairs and into the room when the maid was not in the hall."

"Then," Joe cut in, "he tossed the furniture around himself. He hung the towels on the balcony as if Helga were already here, and he put the envelope—with the money Helga'd gotten at his request and with her fingerprints on it—in the room."

"The set-up," Karl now added, "was to make it appear that Chuck was blackmailing Helga. He'd supposedly come that morning to get ten thousand dollars from her, but she'd only brought five. The five thousand she'd actually gotten at her husband's request, once again. So Chuck and Helga were to have fought, with Chuck throwing her over the balcony."

Helga turned white at hearing this. And Parker, giving up his post by the door, walked to the center of the room to ask, "But who?"

Joe thought he understood the cryptic question and responded, "Evidently Halsey planned to let Helga in when she arrived, and, we suspect, then knock her unconscious. When Chuck came and knocked, Halsey simply wouldn't answer the door. As soon as Chuck gave up and left, Halsey would have thrown Helga's body over the balcony, intending for the fall to kill her. Then he would slip out of the apartment himself by the stairwell."

"But how?"

Joe shrugged. "Here we can only surmise. I imagine—in light of what you told us about those balcony railings—that Halsey was trying to fix some more of the scene. He probably was pushing on the railing, trying to bend it or break it loose to give the appearance of a violent struggle."

"And in the process," Karl put in, "the railing came off with less effort than he'd expected. He was probably off balance and lost control."

"So," Joe concluded, "over he went."

"Then, when Helga knocked, and when Chuck knocked," Mary Margaret said aloud, as if concluding to herself, "no one was there to let either of them in. They never were in here."

"And since they had come for illicit purposes," Karl explained, "they left secretively, as well."

"And," Joe added, "in part because the back side of this building is relatively secluded and, in part by happenstance, no one came upon Halsey's body for perhaps half an hour."

Parker walked slowly around the room now, considering this argument and glancing from the door to the balcony and back to the door. "It's awfully complicated," he suggested.

"It was a complicated plot," Joe replied.

"And it's all circumstantial," the officer went on. "And . . . and so complicated."

"In using the scientific method," Joe continued, "if one can eliminate all the plausible alternative solutions save one, and if that remaining one is itself plausible, and if it fits the facts, however simple or complicated it might be, then one's confidence in its accuracy must remain high."

Parker stood looking over the room, scratching his head uncertainly.

"The practical man of the law," Joe said to Karl, "is not persuaded by theory alone either." Turning back to Parker, Joe smiled and added, "I believe, we believe, there is one piece of hard, incontrovertible evidence. And something you said sensitized us to it."

Parker looked up in wonder.

"Remember," Joe went on, "how you rationalized Helga's statement that she'd gotten the money at her husband's request? You said that it was a convenient excuse because he was not alive to refute it. Well, Halsey, in his plot, planned something equally as convenient. It was the note from Helga to Chuck. That was the one thing he had to forge. He probably did a pretty good job of it, too. After all, he'd surely seen her handwriting many times. And once she was dead, she'd not be around to dispute its authenticity."

Joe paused and smiled in triumph before saying, "I expect that a qualified handwriting expert, furnished with that note and samples of both Helga's and her husband's handwriting, would certainly conclude she did not author the note. Perhaps, such an expert could also confirm, although it would no longer be necessary to do so, that there is strong evidence that Halsey was the author. And that, I believe, is your hard, incontrovertible evidence that binds the whole into a tight, believable explanation."

There was a moment of silence and, admittedly, one of considerable relief. Then Helga sprang from the sofa and ran to hug the stunned Birnoff.

"Herr Professor!" she gushed. "You have Helga's life saved, yes? You were wonderful!" And, turning to the others in the room, she asked, "Wasn't he wonderful?" Then she pressed an exaggeratedly amorous kiss on his cheek.

Joe blinked in surprise and, as his face turned a red that

nearly matched the vivid lip-print on his cheek, he broke into a huge grin.

The ever-poised Karl, however, interrupted the moment of surprise that followed with the laconic assessment, "You may have won the girl, Joseph, but I believe I came out on top in our little wager. However, I'm late for my tennis match, so you can sign the stock over to me at dinner."

Joe blinked again, but this time because a very different thought was taking shape in his head. "Whatever do you mean?" he asked.

"I believe my meaning to be quite plain," Karl replied, moving toward the door. "Halsey clearly had an economic motive to eliminate Helga, and probably the best economic motive for murder in the whole lot of those involved. All his millions and his publishing empire would surely have been at risk had he tried to divorce Helga. Or had she tried to divorce him, for that matter. Murder was his only way out.

"And, on my second point--the one about how it had to be someone of low moral character—well, Halsey was, after all, simply a pornographer. Can there be a lower moral character than that?"

Joe was stunned. He rocked back on his heels and then forward again on his toes. Then he saw that his friend was about to get away out the door, so he dashed—if that's a fair verb for a short, plump man's execution of it—after him. And Joe shouted, "But wait! That's preposterous. It wasn't even a murder in the first place. And in the second place . . ."

Joe's counterargument and Karl's rebuttal trailed off down the hall, drowned in part by the chorus of laughter among those they left behind.